P9-CRV-665

SERIOUSLY

Also by Lucia Nevai

NORMAL

STAR GAME

SERIOUSLY

A Novel

Lucia Nevai

LITTLE, BROWN AND COMPANY
New York   Boston

Copyright © 2004 by Lucia Nevai

All rights reserved. No part of this book may be reproduced in any form or by any electronic or mechanical means, including information storage and retrieval systems, without permission in writing from the publisher, except by a reviewer who may quote brief passages in a review.

Little, Brown and Company
Time Warner Book Group
1271 Avenue of the Americas, New York, NY 10020
Visit our Web site at www.twbookmark.com

First Edition

The characters and events in this book are fictitious. Any similarity to real persons, living or dead, is coincidental and not intended by the author.

Some chapters of this novel were previously published in slightly different form: "Eleanor" (*The Iowa Review*), "Rocky & Helen" and "Glorine" (*The New England Review*), "Dave L. Garson & His Wife, Flo," "Plain Glen" and "Fran" (*Blueline*), "Henry" (*Fiction*), "Viola" (*Phantasmagoria*).

Carolyn Kizer's "The Blessing" (excerpt) is from *Yin*. Copyright © 1984 by Carolyn Kizer. Reprinted with the permission of BOA Editions, Ltd. Theodore Roethke's "She" (excerpt) is from *Words for the Wind*. Reprinted with the permission of Doubleday, a division of Random House, Inc.

Library of Congress Cataloging-in-Publication Data

Nevai, Lucia.
   Seriously / Lucia Nevai. — 1st ed.
      p.   cm.
   ISBN 0-316-74693-2
   1. Young women — Fiction. I. Title.
   PS3564.E848S47   2004
   813'.54 — dc22

                                                2003020586

         10 9 8 7 6 5 4 3 2 1

Book Design by Robert G. Lowe

Q-MB

Printed in the United States of America

For Nondor

Daughter-my-mother,
you have observed my worst.
Holding me together at your expense
has made you burn cool.

—From "The Blessing," Carolyn Kizer

SERIOUSLY

Rocky & Helen

The local insurance agency was housed in a former ice cream stand at the edge of Highway 6 south of the hamlet of Dustin, New York. All four glass sides as well as the roof were angled slightly—intentionally, though the angles chosen looked dumb and unprofessional, as if a three-year-old had tried and failed to draw a square. It was my plan to get insurance there. First I needed something to insure.

I was turning the old feed store into an art gallery—on a shoestring, a loan from my sister. She was the successful one, a television producer in Los Angeles. Once again, she'd jumped at a chance to help me get established somewhere doing something. We were both worried about me. "Incorporate," she said. I did.

It took a while—I couldn't decide on a name. Being in love seemed to slow everything down. I kept sighing and daydreaming and thinking about the last time and looking forward to the next time. When I thought of a name, I ordered a sign. That took a while, too. A man had to design the letters, carve them in wood, then gild the whole thing. Next on my list was the floor.

The floor was worn and stained and buckled in places, but it was a beautiful floor, made of wide planks of red oak. I called up a couple of friends I'd met on the Lower East Side of Manhattan who did floors. I offered to trade them the work for a week in the country. We agreed that I would pay their bus fare up and back, cook for them, and put them up. They would sand, smooth, fill in the cracks, and coat the oak with three layers of polyurethane. We scheduled a week, then they didn't show. This happened twice. The second time, they didn't even call. I drove to Wickley to meet their bus and they didn't get off. I sat there at the bus stop after the bus was gone, looking at the iridescent phallic-shaped oil stain on the concrete in the loading zone.

Back at home, I went through the Yellow Pages. All the local floor guys were busy, too busy for months even to come by and give me an estimate. I dropped the floor project and decided to concentrate on insurance.

My sister told me to insure locally. She said the hometown agent considered you a traitor if you didn't, and if you did, he would really go to bat for you when there was a good-size claim. "Insure everything," my sister said. "I don't want you calling me up for another loan when some farmer walks in, trips over his own shoelaces, ends up in traction, and you get sued."

"Do you really think that's likely?" I said. It was the wrong moment to be sarcastic. A silence hummed in the wires between our coasts—her way of letting me know she was patiently reviewing past investments in me that had turned out badly—a car I wrecked, three years of college tuition, an apartment in New York City.

"Do your only sister a favor, Tamara," she said. "Take yourself seriously for once." I promised her I was serious. I would get insurance.

It was August and too hot to wear anything but shorts. I should have stayed in my cutoffs and flip-flops. I should have driven the three hundred yards down Highway 6 to the insurance agency, but I was new and out of place and I assumed I should look business-like, so I put on a dress and I walked.

To enter the agency was to fill up the only available three square feet of floor space. The air conditioner was loudly generating ice-cold air, which had the unrefreshing effect of cooling the cigarette smoke produced by two apparently overworked agents, man and wife. Their steel desks had been pushed together in the center to form a work island. Around the perimeter were stacks of ancient cartons marked 1976 A–F and so on.

The woman, thin with gray hair, was entering data slowly on a word processor, a fresh cigarette busily burning in a huge chrome ashtray filled with butts. The man, stocky, though equally gray, toyed with his cigarette as he pored over a stack of mail. This was Rocky, no doubt. The little red and white sign at the north end of town read:

BE SHUR, IN-SURE. SHURBERRY'S STATE FARM INSURANCE.

ASK FOR "ROCKY."

"Excuse me," I said, after standing there for several minutes.

Rocky Shurberry checked his wristwatch, took a puff on his cigarette, coughed. Without looking up from the mail, he said in a deep whiskey voice, "Helen?" Helen punched in a few more numbers. She reached for the burning cigarette, brought it to her lips, and inhaled deeply, replacing it in the ashtray, bull's-eye, without taking her eyes from the computer screen. If they were both blind, I would have concluded that they were functioning at their optimum.

"Yes?" she said, finally breaking her concentration.

"Someone's here."

"I'm trying to finish this," she said.

"I'm processing the mail here," he said, shuffling through the stack of four or five items paper-clipped to their envelopes.

The telephone rang. Rocky went back to the mail, his brow in three even furrows. Helen leisurely removed a new cigarette from a leather-encased pack, lit it with the tip of the one in the ashtray, and stamped out the butt. The phone was on its fifth ring when she answered.

"Shurberry's State Farm," she said. "Could you hold, please?" She covered the receiver with her hand. "Rocky," she said. "I can't do everything. I've only got two arms and two legs. Now, do you want to take this call or help this girl?"

With an air of hopelessness, Rocky tossed the mail aside and reached for the phone. Helen removed her narrow-framed glasses and turned to face me at last. "Can I help you?" she asked, though the look on her face said, *Can I hurt you?*

"I want to get prices," I said, and read to Helen from the page of notes I'd taken on the phone with my sister, mentioning fire, theft, and full liability coverage, either as a floater or as a second separate policy. Helen's features became steadily more sober and pinched as I read. Rocky interrupted me.

"The Chuzzners," he said to her. "Do they have term?"

She swiveled in her chair to face him. "Can't you see I'm busy?"

"I'd get the file myself," he said, "but every time I go over to your side of the office, you snap at me for getting in your way and slowing you down and I don't know what all."

"Tell them to call back."

"It's an emergency," he said.

"I just hope this isn't the straw that breaks the camel's back," Helen muttered.

This elicited a companion mutter from Rocky, "I'm going to have to get a professional secretary in here," which silenced Helen, though something like hatred was expelled from her ears in palpable streaks.

"Provide the spelling," she ordered.

"Chuzzner. C-H-U-Z—"

"Write it down."

"Hold on, please," he told the party, laying the phone on the desk, lighting a cigarette. He fished around for a scrap of paper in his nearly empty wastebasket, taking time to read both sides of each scrap. The first piece he selected was too small for his large handwriting—he only got to the N. The second scrap was large enough both to contain the eight capital letters and to sail through the air, his solution when Helen would not reach for it.

Helen read the scrap. "Ask them the policy number," she said, studying the spelling.

Rocky asked. "They don't know," he reported.

"Tell them they should have the policy number written down by the telephone with all the other emergency numbers: fire, police, doctor, ek-cetra." While Rocky was relaying this information, Helen turned to me and said, "Do people really think we know their policy numbers by heart?"

Rocky began to cough. He held the receiver to his chest to muffle the sound and coughed in a long, loud, entirely personal interlude. Helen watched over the rims of her glasses as if she were timing him. Rocky got out a handkerchief, wiped the moisture from his lips, poked the wet, lumpy thing in a rear pocket. The voice on the line had risen in anger—I could hear it from where I was standing. "Tell them we can't locate the document presently," Helen said.

Rocky told them. "Never fails," he said, hanging up. "You try to help people and they turn on you."

"It's what I've been telling you for thirty years," she said. There was peace between them on this point. "So who died?"

"Al."

"Al died?" She and Rocky looked each other through and through, enjoying a private joke of long standing. "See if you can help *her*," Helen said as if it were a challenge. "She doesn't know what she wants."

"I do, too!" I said. My ears were getting red the way they did when my sister lectured me.

"Hold on, calm down, just relax," Rocky said. He folded his hands on his paperwork and swiveled toward me in his swivel chair. I felt as if I was about to receive pastoral counseling. "What is it you need?"

"I want prices. I'm starting an art gallery in the old feed store."

"You're the new girl," Rocky informed me. *Girl.* I was pushing thirty. "What kind of coverage?" I read again from my page of notes. His expression grew befuddled. "Let me see that," he said, reaching for the paper in my hand. I gave it to him. "Whose writing is this?"

"Mine."

"There is no such thing as a liability floater," he said scornfully. "You get the blanket liability with the policy."

"Who told you we had a liability floater?" Helen asked with indignation.

"My sister," I answered idiotically.

"Look, miss," Rocky said. "You're going to sell what—the

Mona Lisa?" He and Helen both erupted in long, phlegmy laughing fits.

Helen wiped her eyes. "Where is your husband at?" she asked to humiliate me.

"If she had one, she don't no more," Rocky told her. Single girls never settle on the crossroads, I learned from Henry Storey, who owned the antiques store next to me.

"Well, how did you intend to pay for this insurance?" Helen asked, as if only men had money.

"What do you care as long as the premium is paid?" I said.

"We screen everybody," Helen said. "To write a bad policy costs us. And the company don't like to see a lot of bad policies from one agent. Do they, Rocky?"

"No, they do not," he said without looking up. In the margin of my notepaper he had drawn the word THEFT in box capitals and was now shading each letter. Perhaps he had wanted to be a commercial artist.

"And what exactly is it you want to insure, anyhow?" Helen asked, blinking rapidly to brace herself against the poverty of my reply.

For once, I was ready with a good answer. "My Nikons are worth two thousand dollars."

"Two thousand, Helen," Rocky said. Helen stopped blinking and inched toward me between the desk and the cartons, as if to get closer to that amount of money. "How much rent do you pay Shirley?" she asked.

"Three-fifty a month."

"You should have asked us. We could have done better for you," Helen said. "We know of a few rentals, all better than that place you're in. Do you have an appraisal for the cameras?"

"Yes."

"Rocky, you've got to go down there," Helen ordered.

He reared back from his lettering, cocking his head to one side in admiration.

"Well, does she know we close for lunch?" he asked.

"We close at twelve," Helen told me. "Rocky will come down after lunch," Helen said. "He needs to write up your full replacement value."

"Fine," I said. I was free until three. Henry Storey was taking me bottle digging that afternoon. He had stumbled on a cache of antique garbage buried in a field nearby—he wouldn't say where. "There's bottle collectors in this town who'd like to get their hands on this stuff," he said. He'd showed me a pale blue-green mason jar recovered from the site, so old there were dozens of tiny bubbles trapped in the glass. "Worth money," he said, holding it up to the light for me.

Rocky and Helen locked up for lunch, climbed into their little nondescript sedan, and drove home—across the highway.

I walked back to the crossroads. I dragged my feet. I felt transparent: a girl with long legs and no history, solemn, detached, unproductive. Frothy, spermy Queen Anne's lace flowered like fireworks along the ditch.

Back in my gallery, I came to an obvious conclusion: insurance was premature. I didn't want Rocky in there estimating my full replacement value until the floors were done, the walls were painted, and the recessed lighting installed. I looked up the Shurberry residence in the phone book—no number. I called Information—they were unlisted. I made a little sign, CLOSED DUE TO HEAT, and taped it to the front door.

I went into my back room, took off the dress, and pulled on my

cutoffs. I felt like myself again. I made a tomato sandwich, then flopped down on my bed, reached under the pillow for Boz's worn black T-shirt, and draped it over my face. I loved his smell. There was a foresty cosmetics element, probably aftershave; a male element, probably sweat; and something invisible and powerfully appealing, the essence of Boz. Three more days before our next motel afternoon. I tossed from side to side, arching my back. I could drive myself crazy this way, but this afternoon I didn't want to, so I sat up and shook it off. This, not art, was the real business of my life, this slow, riveting revelation of a sexual self, unfolded to me tryst by tryst by a man who felt the same thing happening to him. Boz had given me his grandfather's gold pocket watch as a token of love, but because there were people in and around Wickley who actually knew that watch by sight, I wasn't allowed to wear it where it could be seen. True, he was still married. But wasn't a token supposed to be something that could be seen? I needed a gesture from him. I needed to feel sure.

I heard Rocky drive up, knock on the front door, ring the buzzer for a full sixty seconds, pound on the display window, ring the buzzer again, call out, knock on the glass, and finally leave.

Henry came to the back door a little after three. His appearance was always eccentric, but now, with two shovels over his shoulder, a large burlap bag hanging down his back, and an old bent-up gray fedora shading his eyes, he looked mythic. "Hey, I want a hat, too," I said. He went next door and found a companion fedora that was too big for my head, so he took it and gave me his.

"Do you think you could bring us a beer?" he asked. I stuck a bottle into each of my back pockets. We tramped down the hill behind our stores. The streambed was low, down to a trickle. We followed it south a ways to the giant culvert under County Route 1, big enough to walk through. It was cool and dark inside. A shallow pool of dark water had collected. Henry edged his way over the stones.

"Know what?" he said, his voice echoing. "Don't slip."

I wasn't paying much attention to where exactly we were going. I climbed the hill behind Henry. He stopped and jabbed his spade into the field and started to dig. There we were, not a hundred feet from the State Farm Insurance office.

Helen saw us first. Her mouth was going a mile a minute as she and Rocky edged their way between the cartons for a better look. My first reflex was to hide. I tried to dig with my back to them, my face in the shadow of the fedora. I felt as if I'd been playing hooky, as if Rocky might pick up the phone right there and then to call my sister, saying, "She's goofing off. She's not getting the insurance from me you told her to get."

"What's eating them?" Henry said.

"I just stood them up," I said.

"That's rich," he said. "Oh boy, is that rich. They have even less of a notion than you about how to run a business." He went back to his digging.

Henry unearthed a beautiful cobalt blue bottle, cylindrical, with a silver cap. I found a tiny brown one with half the label still intact: Carter's Little Liver Pills.

I was brushing the dirt off the lip when I saw the red Mercury. Boz was driving slowly by the gallery, hoping for a glimpse of me, his red taillights brightening with desire with each tap of the brakes. I stood riveted to the hillside in a state of unwise exhilaration that began in the soles of my feet and ended in the tips of my hair, watching the red car disappear over the hill. I opened our beers.

SERIOUSLY

Henry found twenty-eight bottles and I found twelve. Rocky and Helen stayed with us, chain-smoking shoulder to shoulder at the window. Every time I looked up, Helen's mouth was still going. They looked so flat, gray, and stale, trapped in their marriage behind the glass, that I felt a rush of tenderness. I hoped the Chuzzners weren't sitting by the phone.

Nora

Nothing about my sister Nora suggested a link with anything as lumpy, bland, or unproductive as a family from the Midwest. This was her strength. And once I could get over wanting to feel related to her, it was mine.

Even deep down, Nora was an extrovert. She was all surface, shiny and bright, like a valuable one-of-a-kind automobile ready for a car show, clean engine and all. She'd redone herself along the lines of what women in her industry considered feminine. Her teeth were whitened, lips enlarged, biceps built, abdominal muscles flattened, nails extended and flawlessly polished, hair dyed, bangs shagged to the side like a television anchor. She had the tan. She had the jewels. She wasn't manufactured to reflect, and nothing she'd undergone by way of customizing had offered even the most marginal reward for introspection. She burned through seventeen-hour California days without breaking a sweat or losing track. She was all business. In the Midwest they referred to a woman like Nora as a dynamo. There was a negative nuance meaning "get out of her way."

The fall after Nora set me up in Dustin, she began to ask about our spending the holidays together. I wondered if she was ready to talk about it—what had happened to our family. All Nora would admit was that one May when I was seventeen, I got on a bus in the middle of the night and rode to Chicago, where she was in college, because our family had died in a fire.

"Is Janice helpful?" Nora asked when I arrived in L.A. at Christmas.

Janice had been Nora's sorority sister at Northwestern. Janice married an attorney and settled in Wickley, the elite town in upstate New York that his family had founded and still ran. Apparently Janice had not been that excited to hear from my sister. She agreed reluctantly to help me find housing, then palmed the job off on her husband, Boz.

"Minimally," I said.

I chose the word carefully. I wanted to end the subject because I was now the husband's mistress. There was always a secret like this when I visited Nora.

Nora noticed the word. She cocked her head at it. I worried for a moment. Later I heard her use it on the phone in the same context, "minimally helpful." She had cocked her head at it to incorporate it. In her case, it made her money. This was the difference between us.

She left the house at six A.M. and returned in the evening at eight. I spent my days looking out her windows, sunning myself on her decks, jogging past the beautiful homes in her fancy neighborhood.

Evenings we watched the shows she made. I very much appreciated the six million telephone calls behind every bright, fast-moving half hour. But perhaps Nora's shows were more fun to make than to watch. The actual viewing experience was like being hooked up to an IV of mindless drivel. Nora was proudest of the new laugh track. These were younger, bawdier, more racially mixed voices. It was something she'd fought for.

I kept thinking about the fire and waiting for Nora to bring it up. There were so many questions, so many things to say. I assumed the invitation to come for Christmas meant that Nora was ready. It didn't. The past two Christmases she had worked. This one she had off. She didn't know anyone to spend Christmas with except me.

On Christmas Eve she wanted to watch *The Grinch* together. "Should I make popcorn?" I asked. My question was loaded with significance. It was a family tradition, the only happy one. "Sure," she said. I nuked some. At her request, I left off the chemical topping. It wasn't quite like getting out the old kettle, unscrewing the jar of Orville Reddenbacker, and melting real butter in the baby cast-iron skillet, but still, the sound of two hundred small organic explosions probably did us both good.

We watched, then we opened gifts. I worried about mine to her. It was about it.

She whistled "Material Girl" as she slid off the ribbon. I watched her neatly unfold the gift wrap at the Scotch-taped ends. I was nervous. I didn't want to cause her too much surprise emotion. I had made her a black-and-white 5 x 7 enlargement of the only surviving snapshot of our family. It was taken in summer in front of the house. It was overexposed, so it looked as if it had been taken forty years ago, not fourteen. There was our home, the pleasant two-story bungalow on Mayfair Street in Watertown, South Dakota. There was the big oak tree that shaded the front yard. There was the hedge that separated our yard from the neighbors'.

When I went into the darkroom to copy this little dog-eared snapshot, my whole body shook. Not trembled, shook—the head-to-toe shakes of someone dying of malaria. The noise of disaster thundered in my ears. If I had not—on a whim—slipped this loose snapshot into the pages of a book I was reading to mark my place fourteen years ago, there would be no remaining record of us.

In my travels, the snapshot got bent. When I copied it for Nora, I took out the crack across the house. It had an unsettling way of denying the family's existence, like the diagonal slash in the international signals for what is forbidden: no parking, no smoking, no walking. A gauzy white streak remained where I dodged in the background of the print. It looked as if the whole family had just arrived in heaven, still sharing the ghostlike house behind them as a common memory.

The picture was back-side up in Nora's lap. She was so meticulous, the wrapping paper looked unused. She turned it over. No gasp. I was glad. She held the thing at arm's length, figuring the cost of the mat—white raw silk—and the frame—gilded oak. Then she held it up close, fascinated with how much she'd changed.

In the snapshot, we three sisters stand like stair steps in front of Dad and Mom. Nora is eighteen. It's the summer before she goes away to Northwestern on a full scholarship. She's confident, dazzling. Her smile beams victory, like the smiles of fighter pilots after they've landed, presidents after they've been elected, Miss Americas as they're crowned. I know I will be rich, her smile says. It's the last time Nora is taller than I am. Once she left home, I felt free to shoot up to my natural height. As long as she was there, I was holding back.

Mom's face is turned three-quarters away. Her arms fall straight to her sides like a normal person, but her hands curl up like dead leaves. Mom is English and stoic, big-boned with a broad, bold, beautiful face. If I try to imagine the terrors she routinely experienced, I am ashamed of the universe.

Dad is the handsome Swede. His eyes look down on Cynthia. She's only seven, but his hands rest on her shoulders as if, without her, he couldn't even stand up. Cynthia is docile and selfless, with Dad's good nature and Mom's good skin. Everything she knows and loves in the world is right there in the picture. Like a pet, she was happiest when she calmed us all down and held us together.

Something is shining in the hedge. It's the chrome handlebar of Cynthia's two-wheeler. Dad was helping her learn to ride. That was the reason the picture was taken. To celebrate. After an hour of falling down, of brushing off her little scraped palms and rubbing the bruises on her little banged knees, she did it. She found the beautiful sudden speed in the pedals, the velocity that freed the uprightness in the bicycle. Her fearful side-to-side wobble narrowed to a waver and off she went. Dad ran after her, his arms reaching toward her waist, ready to catch her should she fall. But she kept going. Down the sidewalk, going, going, going.

What would Nora think of me? I look lost, out of place, ignored by both parents. Trapped between big sister and little, I inherited Mom from Nora, gave it my all for a couple of years, then passed her on to Cynthia. My attributes—Dad's Swedish cheekbones and long legs—count for nothing here. Only my dog, sitting at my feet, seems to worship me. My chin's a blur as I turn to the photographer. Anyone can see that the look in my eye is desire, a comfortable, habitual, reciprocal desire for the man clicking the shutter. I was with him when the fire broke out.

"Mother looks fine," Nora said. There was a note of accusation, as if I had been exaggerating all this time.

"After you left, she changed."

"People don't change *that* much," Nora said.

"*She* did."

"What'd she do?" Nora said.

"She couldn't sleep and she made the bedroom really weird."

"Maybe it just seemed weird to you," Nora said. "Maybe it wasn't your style."

Mom had installed a brass security rod that they advertised on our late-night local television station. With the flick of a lever, this rod prevented any door from opening more than three inches. Mom nailed black rubber welcome mats over the windows to stop the voices. Her bed became a psycho four-poster that looked part science fiction, part sadomasochistic hospital ward. The box spring was supported by four little pillars made of concrete blocks. Sheets of black construction plastic hung like shower curtains from copper tubing suspended around all four sides of the bed. She was trying to stop the rays.

"What are you folks building over there?" the hardware store man had asked me. I walked past his store on my way home from school.

"Beats me," I said, finding the neutral tone and the casual shrug that would bore him sufficiently to make him look elsewhere for information. I was already an expert at pretending we were normal.

Every day after school I forced myself to go upstairs to see if she was alive. Her bedroom door was closed. "Mom?" I called in a soft, daughterlike voice. No answer. I knocked in a manner I knew to be friendly, respectful, servile. No answer. I took a deep breath and turned the knob. "Mom, are you okay?" I said in a loud, ordinary, innocent whisper. She was plagued by sleeplessness. All night she lay awake. In case she had finally managed to doze off, I didn't want to be accused of waking her up unjustifiably. Yet I'd learned to announce myself. If I just opened the door without saying anything, she screamed for a while. I opened it one inch at a time until it hit the barrier.

"Close. The. Door," she said on good days, and I heard and appreciated in her voice the immense struggle she was making not to scream at me.

"After you left," I said to Nora, "she quit her job. Things really went downhill after that."

"Mom was a spoiled brat," Nora said. "She didn't want to work."

"Her letter of resignation was weird," I said.

"What'd it say?"

"It said she was tired of spending half her time in other people's offices trapping the negative pre-said."

"She was pulling their leg, for Christ's sake," Nora said. "She was smarter than everybody. She was always pulling someone's leg."

"Did you happen to read the investigator's report?" I said.

The insurance people had given Nora the original. She sent me a copy. It was 290 pages long.

"Who has time to read?" Nora said.

The report described windows that had been nailed shut. Not hastily. Meticulously. With twenty-four to thirty nails per window, evenly spaced, driven in to the head. It analyzed debris that pointed to explosives. It identified the presence of a string of two-gallon containers of gasoline in closets and cupboards, planted to accelerate the blaze. All doors appeared to have been locked. The gas range was obliterated. The report summarized no fewer than seventeen unrelated proofs of arson. Everyone in the house had been sleeping when the blaze began. The bodies were found under the beds, where they had crawled to get away from the smoke.

"They say it was suspicious," I said.

"Look, T.J.," Nora said. She was using her big-sister voice. "If the insurance company calls it arson, they don't have to pay."

"Nora," I said. "Mom burned them up."

"She smoked," Nora said. "Did you know Mom smoked?"

I was shocked. I couldn't answer. Mom didn't smoke.

"She smoked in bed sometimes. The house burned down."

Like many self-made people, Nora assumed that her success in the workplace entitled her to instant status as an authority on everything. "Do you know what the most amazing thing in this picture is?" she said.

"What?"

"I weigh the same now as I did then." She unfolded the hinged easel and placed the photo on her lamp table.

Just in case she'd missed one of the main points of the gift, I explained it. "I made that for you," I said. "I enlarged the photograph, chose the mat, and cut the frame."

"You did? You made it yourself?" She was newly pleased at her recent investment in me.

"Here." She handed me a book. "I didn't have time to wrap it."

How to Make Ends Meet and Never Live Beyond Your Means, read the title. The subtitle was *365 Creative Ways to Cut Back, Save & Go Without.* "Thank you," I said. The two words *go without* set off in my head an immediate compensational series of erotic fantasies, as if I had to remind myself of the big how-to I knew better than Nora. I thumbed through the book in a lackluster fashion to show a measure of appreciation.

"There's a bookmark in there," she said in case one of the main points of the gift was lost on me. I found it in the chapter on saving. It was a personal check from Nora to me for a thousand dollars.

"I made that myself," she said.

"Thank you very much," I said, sincere this time. I gave her a hug to make up for pouting a bit over the cheesy book. Who cared if we felt like sisters or not. Ever since my bus trip to Chicago the night of the fire, Nora had saved me whenever I asked her to—whether she knew what she was doing or not. We said merry Christmas and watched the news.

Before I flew back to New York, Nora promised to come east for a visit. "I'd like to see Janice again," she said. I choked for a while. She poured me a glass of sparkling water with no insight whatsoever. There were advantages to her pathological extroversion.

Within days after my return, the Writers Guild voted to strike the networks. Nora called in the scabs and wrote shows herself. She lost track of me. Her voice on the answering machine sounded distracted and nearly hysterical.

In March I got the call. It came as all such calls come, in the middle of the night. She was hurt, they said, in a car accident.

I flew out to L.A., rented a car, and drove to her bedside at Beverly Hills Medical Center. Hurt was a euphemism. She was DOA when they brought her in. Until I saw her lying there, rigid with plaster, dripping with IVs, choked with a ventilator, slit with transfusion tubes, surrounded by monitors that hummed and beeped because she couldn't, I didn't know that I loved her more than anything on earth.

Her eyes were closed. I lifted the sheet and found her hand. "Nora, Nora, Nora," I said. Her eyes opened.

"Nora, you're going to be fine," I said. I found the bossy, cocksure tone of voice she'd always used on me and threw it at her. "We're going to make you good as new. We're going to get you out of here as soon as we can." A tear rolled out of one eye.

"Do you hurt?" I asked.

She squeezed my hand twice for yes, the way they'd taught her. "Where?"

Another tear.

"Everywhere?"

Twice for yes. She wept when I massaged the soft pink soles of her feet. It was as if I'd learned a little reflexology at yoga class just in time to help her heal.

"I love you," I said. I was ashamed—it was the first time I'd ever said those three words to her. I'd almost missed the chance to say them at all. She told me she loved me, too, squeezing my hand three times.

"I have to go now," I said when, once again, they ordered me out of the ICU. Two big nurses were dragging me backward through the opening in Nora's curtain. Our eyes stayed locked even as the great steel door slammed shut.

Fifteen medical professionals, twelve machines, and six drugs were circulating around and through Nora to make her live. All were large and white, with the potential for error, defeat, infection. It was humbling to think that before Nora's car accident, her little size-six body accomplished all these functions and processes with no breaks, no thanks.

The first day, she improved dramatically. I took the credit and was elated. The second day, she slipped back into a coma, not answering my voice, not squeezing my hand, not opening her eyes. I took the blame—I'd exhausted her. I did some quick, hypocritical emotional housekeeping and taught myself to pray. On day three, I made her laugh.

That night I found a drug dealer at Blockbuster and loaded up on tranquilizers. I hadn't done this for a while. Funny how easily it all came back.

In a week the head nurse said Nora was well enough to move into a private room.

"Hi, Tammy," she said, clear as day. She hadn't called me that since she was twelve. I ran out into the hall to tell her nurse she had spoken. When the nurse arrived at Nora's bedside to see and hear for herself, Nora suddenly feigned sleep. The nurse eyed me critically—I'd wasted her time, I'd exaggerated, perhaps even lied.

As soon as her nurse left, Nora said, "Tammy, Tammy, Tammy, Tammy, Tammy."

I understood. "You don't like her, do you," I said. Once for no. She had exhausted herself. She was back to hand squeezing.

I peeked through the curtain the next time the nurse went in to change Nora's IV and witnessed an incompetent, far-sighted depressive who looked at the floor as she jabbed and jabbed up and down Nora's vein, her face registering no effect whatsoever as Nora flinched. I flew at the head nurse, screaming, waving my arms, clawing the air with my fingernails, demanding a change. There were no other beds available. I insisted. She moved Nora into the children's wing.

"Thank you," Nora said to me.

I hired a private nurse named Hazel to sit beside Nora all night, screening everything and everyone. Hazel had washed and dried Nora's hair, which was very necessary, but she had styled it in pigtails tied with Day-Glo green yarn. I had forgotten to mention that Nora was thirty-two.

"My God! You look like Joy Wantaugh!" I said to Nora when Hazel was gone. Nora stuck out her little tongue at the mere mention of her third-grade enemy.

"Did you try to stop her?" I asked.

Nora nodded yes.

"How?"

Nora spoke her first full sentence. "I shit."

I asked more questions this time when I interviewed private night nurses. Juanita was young and round and confident. She smelled faintly of cornmeal and cumin. She loved television. They watched it together. In her warm, passionate, lilting Mexican accent, demonstrating a great understanding of human nature but no understanding of personal pronouns, Juanita summarized the content of Nora's competitors' daytime shows.

"The lonely woman, he finds love with the young boy who mows the lawn, but the husband—she hired the boy to do it, because she has a mistress."

Rivalry flowed in Nora's veins again, adding extra oxygen and glucose, improving her complexion.

When Nora was talking more and walking a little, I began to bring in her business clothes. Juanita had a heyday, dressing up Nora like an executive, brooches, watch, rings and all. Nora's assistant was showing up at nine with a miniature handheld digital television monitor so Nora could review her shows. Juanita caught a few continuity errors. Nora's assistant began to worry about her job security. Nora was calling me Tamara again. The day she started bossing me around, I knew I could go home.

I went into her room to say good-bye. She and Juanita were

watching TV. I stood beside her for a moment. She wouldn't look at me. I wanted a real farewell. I had always wanted a real farewell. As far back as I could remember, Nora was always leaving me behind, charging out into life without a wave or a hug good-bye. She went everywhere first—to school, to college, to Europe, to L.A.

When she got where she was going and made a success of herself, that's when she sent for me. She absorbed the assault of the world for me. I absorbed the assault of home for her. She let me share her thick skin. I reminded her of who we were. Nora, Nora, Nora. I tried to hug her. Her body stayed rigid, turned three-quarters away.

"Safe trip," she said. "Call when you get there."

"You brat," Juanita said to her. Juanita rolled up the *TV Guide* and used it to bonk Nora playfully on the head. I was shocked and exhilarated to see Nora accept her reproof. "Show some love—he's your only sister," Juanita said with that soothing Mexican inflection I would forever after associate with intimacy at its most natural, wrong pronouns and all.

Nora looked at me obediently. Her eyes grew sad—a shock for me—as if I were our joint past, the whole wasted, sorrowful thing. Her smile deepened in the unnatural exercise of reflection. We hugged until her stitches hurt. Her hand found mine and squeezed it three times.

❖

I had saved two tranquilizers for the plane. I wanted to get off them as soon as possible. I took my two in the airport at the gate and waited to relax, but instead, as I always did when I left Nora, I fell apart. Thirty-five thousand feet in the air—what a place to become unhinged. I drank to stop hyperventilating, then watched drunkenly as my ego continued flying east in thirty-five thousand pieces.

We landed at JFK on Saturday morning. They had had snow, but it was a week old and dirty. In the long-term parking lot, I couldn't find my Saab. Walking past row after row of snow-covered cars in the cold, dragging my noisy wheeled suitcase behind me, I felt the warmth and brightness of California, the blue skies, the cumin-scented emotional wholeness of Juanita, the first loving exchange between any family member and me—all of it taking its place in ancient personal history. I cried like an orphan. My nose ran and I let it.

I stopped to smoke. Behind me, hunkered down between SUVs, all but hidden by the drifts, was my little blue Saab. I drove back upstate shaking, afraid it wouldn't look like home, afraid I had changed too much to live there, afraid I would pack up and flee, as usual.

HAMLET OF DUSTIN. The little green sign with one bent corner appeared around the bend on Highway 6. It smiled at me. There was Viola's silhouette at the counter of her filthy luncheonette. I could almost smell the burnt coffee, the ink of her fresh daily *New York Times*. There was Henry in his hat out in back of both our stores, looking for something to take apart and never put back together. Henry's hat, the crushed fedora, worn off the face on the back of the head—the sight of it warmed and charmed me. It sprang from something uncrushable and festive in the human spirit, something that embraced life, however marginal the days and abstinent the nights, something I was here to learn.

Boz

He gave me the things I needed, the first of which was love. It began in May on a humid, fragrant weekday afternoon. I climbed down the steps of the bus into his small, rich town, and Boz was waiting for me. He was wearing something tweedy and lawyerly. He looked responsible and relaxed, confident and civic. He was a man who had enjoyed status even in the womb—for generations, his family had owned and run the town of Wickley. He was also a divided man. He had one green eye and one brown. It was as if they saw and wanted different things from life at the same time. When he saw me, his body made an inaudible sound like the click people refer to when they say, *We clicked.* I was wearing cutoffs, sandals, and a T-shirt. My yellow hair was halfway down my back. One little braid ending with beads fell forward across my cheek.

I had been expecting his wife. She was the one who was supposed to be helping me. This was the first thing I said to him: "I was expecting your wife."

He was gallant. I got used to it the way you get used to the sun on a vacation at the beach. The way he tilted his face toward mine to demonstrate attentiveness. The way he held open a door, yet also guided me through it, two fingertips lightly resting in the center of my back. These were his manners and he used them on everyone. I knew that and I also knew that when he used them on me, he helplessly sent a shiver of erotic promise through his eyes into mine, through his fingertips into my spine.

I needed a job. He found me one. Six weeks later I was fired. To tell him this, I made an appointment with his secretary. She led me down the walnut-paneled hall of the historic brick town house where he practiced law. She seated me in the conference room on the lovely butter-smooth Italian leather sofa. I was wearing my tight jeans and the blue shirt that made my eyes look even bluer. I had put on perfume to tell him the bad news, mascara too. When Boz came in, he left the double doors open and stood between them as if he would soon be leaving. "How's it going?" he asked.

I said, "Fine. Great." There was a silence. I added. "Really great."

"Great," he said. He smiled his safe, civic smile.

"They fired me," I said. "And it's my birthday." I started to cry. He dropped to his knees before me and took my hands in his. He murmured endless things to reassure me, extravagant things in one long run-on sentence, maintaining an avuncular tone, although his eyes were deeply affected by our being so close. I felt sorry for him because he was in love with me and I didn't care. He smelled very good. That was all I would grant him that day—after all, it was my birthday.

I needed a car. He found me a used one, a Saab, in my favorite color, blue. He taught me to drive a stick shift. I had been unfair. I had misconstrued things. I took his goodness for a lack of bravery, his refusal to dominate as a deficiency in testosterone. There was restlessness there, not complacency. In repose, his features suggested defeat more than victory. His eyes were scraped bare by an absence of physical love.

I was staying in the Daley Hotel Bar & Grill. Every night I would look out my window at the parking lot of the bar and see his red car parked at a rakish angle like a spontaneous invitation. I didn't go in, but I thought about it.

The Fourth of July fell on a Saturday. Every year people came for miles to see the town of Wickley's long, elaborate parade. I was standing alone in a gap in the crowd, eating caramel corn when Boz rode by on the Democrats of Wickley float. The float parodied its constituency, featuring people dressed as farmers, artists, wealthy liberals, and minorities. Boz was wearing dark glasses and playing Ray Charles tunes on an upright piano. The singers surrounding him were beautiful young black girls wearing gold necklaces with their names in huge script and tight bicycle shorts. To punctuate a glissando that went all the way up to high G, Boz looked right at me and blew me a kiss. I went upstairs to my hotel room and threw up. I blamed the caramel corn, but I knew it was love.

The next night I was sitting on my hotel bed, watching a pay-per-view movie, when I got a craving for potato chips. I ran across the street to the Grand Union. It was five minutes to nine. Almost no one was left in the store. I found the chips, opened them in the aisle, and ate a few. The bag was fresh. Every chip was salty and crisp. I turned into the pickle aisle. There was Boz, confounded by the huge number of pickles to choose from. We were both speechless. I held a chip up to his lips. He bit it gratefully, looking at me as his lips touched my fingertips. There was salt on both our lips now. It was difficult not to kiss. A bell sounded. A voice on the PA told us to bring our last purchases to checkout register eleven. I left the store, forgetting to pay. As the door closed behind me, the bell sounded again, the PA voice saying, "Would the janitor please come to the pickle aisle with a mop."

All week I looked for him. Up one side of Main Street and down the other. I was dressed to please—in fact, to provoke—in white short shorts and a white shirt undone to the third button. No Boz. By Saturday I had given up. I went for a pedicure. Inside, the waitress from the Co-See Coffee Shop was getting new fingernail extensions, stripes in five shades of blue.

I sat in the soft pink leatherette chair. The girl washed my feet, kneaded my soles, pumiced my heels, clipped my toenails. She held my infant-clean foot gently and brushed the nails with Amazon pink, my choice from the seventy-two polishes lined up like temptations, from white to red. She laid little cotton space makers between my toes and sat me down in front at the window with my feet up to dry.

The beauty salon faced the back of the redbrick town house where Boz practiced law. The back door opened and he came out. It was 4:30 on a Saturday in summer and he was just leaving the office. He sat in his red car—how had I missed it?—staring out the windshield at the parking lot. His face looked sunken and deprived.

I had always seen him from the perspective of the waiting room of his law office, responding in princelike, able ways to civic, legal, municipal concerns. He moved at the center of a fixed, privileged world, arranging, protecting, preserving. His wife, his parents, his brother, his brother's four children, were weekly items on his business calendar, along with his clients, along with his town.

He had at his fingertips everything a man was supposed to want—power, wealth, influence, respect. He had family—the one thing in life I thought would save any soul. Yet he sat alone in his car on a Saturday afternoon, feeling despair.

He turned on the radio. Something there seemed to help—a song, an interview, an NPR show. He drove away, but my toes weren't dry, so I couldn't follow to see where he lived.

I needed a real-estate agent. He found me three. I struck out with the first two, both snobs. I made an appointment to tell him this.

"Try wearing a dress that makes you look rich," he said.

"I don't have any dress like that," I said.

"Are you asking me to buy you one?" he asked, not to criticize but to clarify.

"I'm asking you to steal me one," I said.

Sunday morning he brought it up to my hotel room. My appointment with Shirley Girt of Girt Real Estate was at three. He came at nine. I was watching out the hotel-room window for his red car when he knocked on the door. He had parked at the office, not the bar.

It was Janice's blue-green summer sheath. She was shorter than I was, and her hips were slimmer, so the dress that skimmed her figure stopped to rest at strategic places on mine. "How do I look?" I said. The hem fell halfway up my thigh. All that skin made it hard for him. Twice, he opened his mouth to say something, but nothing came out.

"What do I do with this to look rich?" I said, taking hold of my long yellow hair in a hank, like a caveman who wanted to marry me might.

"Straight back off the forehead in a ponytail," he said.

I sat down at the vanity. "Like so?" I said. I was an instant patrician.

"That's it," he said.

We were looking at each other in the mirror. I felt sick. I was going to say it. "I love you."

His face fell upward into joy. "Darling!" he said, and locked the door.

The bed that had seemed so small to me for weeks became vast. We sprawled there afterward, gazing at the fading peonies on the hotel wallpaper, Boz tracing my bones with his fingertips, kneading the important spot at the back of the neck where the spine flowers into the brain. Our senses were stunned, our ears ringing, as if we'd both been hit in the face with a swinging two-by-four.

He went stumbling back to his life. It was easier for me, because I didn't have one yet. I drove to Mill Street to meet Shirley Girt. Love was mine. Mine, mine, mine—I said the word over and over to myself, because Boz wasn't.

❖

Three afternoons a week we met at the Cloverleaf Motel. Just when room thirty-two began to seem too small, summer turned to fall and we met at the lake cottage that his great extended family had closed up for the season. Now from the bed we could see graceful pine trees with boughs dancing in the wind, stands of slender reeds tinted blond, and water, sparkling, life-giving water that smacked the shore and sucked at the dock and rocked the footings of the little foundationless cottage just enough to keep everything—earth, sky, water, lovers—in tune.

It was the only time I saw Boz at ease. He would rise from the bed, pulling on his slacks, wandering barefoot into the main room in a youthful stupor. A trailing arm would reach into a bowl of apples and take one. He would lounge in the doorway to the porch, gazing through the screen at the water, taking a bite. I could easily imagine the other times, as a boy, as a man, that he'd done just this.

Family portraits in heavy silver frames crowded the mantel. I studied them, looking and listening for the special hubbub of the Boswell family collecting for a swim, preparing for a picnic, rowing toward the dock in the boat at dusk with a bucket of fish, chattering over cocktails. There would be peaches and plums ripening in baskets, wildflowers spilling petals from a vase, the casual bounty and excessive beauty of summer, summer, summer in a house built to celebrate it.

Sometimes when I sat in his lap in the club chair by the fireplace, I asked him to talk about the people in the photos. "Family is a mixed blessing," he said when I told him how lucky he was to have such an old one.

The snapshot of his brother caught him at his best, in a chorus line with his four children, all in bathing suits on the dock, arms linking shoulders, left legs kicking right at the same family angle. Ted was two years older than Boz. He looked fifty and acted twelve. He was a big, rude, bearlike bully with gray shoulder-length hair. In the middle of my first appointment with Boz, Ted barged into the office, unshowered, unshaven, wearing a Hawaiian shirt and unclean shorts. He grunted at me and swiped an envelope of cash off the top of the desk. This, I correctly concluded, was where Boz got his pot. What I didn't know was that Boz paid and paid and paid. Getting Ted out of messes and scrapes was time-consuming, secret, and frequent.

The photograph of their parents had been taken in a garden in Florence. They had movie-star charisma. They looked like the rich in the ballroom scenes in Cary Grant movies. Occasionally I saw them on Wickley's Main Street, entering or exiting the bank. The scale of the Italy photograph brought them down to a manageable size. In person they were too large, too tall, too brisk. He was always gallantly opening doors for her in a way that kept other people waiting. She was always taking his arm to descend a height, even the ludicrous height from the curb to the street.

I asked Boz what they were like. "Monsters," he said.

His case in point was his own portrait at age one. I found it charming, extravagant, playful. He considered it obscene. His mother dressed him in a custom-sewn navy serge suit. He wore a little white shirt, a little red tie. A linen hankie peeked out of the breast pocket in a tiny neat triangle. His eyebrows were beautiful. His forehead was high. His skin, his nose, his chin were perfect. The smile on his face seemed to say, *I'm born to be great.* But Boz was right. His eyes were already starved, their excessive brightness working off a battery that surely drained his spiritual reserves.

His wife was there, too, of course. For a long time I avoided her photo. Then one afternoon I picked it up off the mantel and held it. We were nestled in the overstuffed chair, cheek to cheek. "That's her," he said. She was an icy, lush brunette. Someone had posed Janice against the pine tree—I could see the very tree from our chair. She had a frank, irreverent poise that I aspired to. *I don't care what you see or don't see in me,* her face said. Her black hair was tousled, not purposefully but out of neglect. She wore khaki shorts and a white shirt with some kind of heirloom jewel peeking out at the throat. Her espadrilles invited thoughts about her calves and knees. Smoke from a burning cigarette arose from her right hand.

"So she smokes, too," I said to Boz, because he hated my smoking.

"She quit," he said.

I pointed out the smoke to him. He seemed disturbed. "She was sneaking one," he admitted. "Someone caught her sneaking one and took this picture."

I also pointed out the foot. A man's bare foot was sticking out from behind the tree. "It's a stick," Boz said, but I could see this bothered him, too. He didn't want to admit to himself that he knew so early on that his brother and his wife were lovers.

I put the photograph back on the mantel.

❖

In the Grand Union I saw her in person. She wore suede pants the color of café au lait. Her cream-colored shirt was tailored and silk. Her belt was new and so expensive that it looked as if it were cut from an old saddle. Again her hair was messy. I looked for her part. It was ragged, yet her lipstick was careful and red. Her lips wanted to smoke, to close sensuously around the next white cigarette as someone, a man, lit the tip.

Her eyes cared little for what she saw in this aisle. Her eyes cared little for what she saw in this town, this life. She didn't know about me yet, but she was about to. My legs were longer. Her tits were bigger.

❖

"What was she like in college?" I asked my sister on the phone. They'd spent four years in the same sorority at Northwestern.

"Neurotic."

"Spoiled-neurotic or genetic-neurotic?" I asked.

"Just neurotic," she said. Her tone was impatient, as if I were wasting her time splitting hairs. My sister didn't know what I was talking about. When I was too deep, instead of asking me to explain, she snapped at me, pulling rank for being older, financially secure, and better educated. She never accepted the inequity that her dropout sister was wiser.

"Give me an example," I said to Nora.

"She came to college with a ton more stuff than everyone else. The first night she got drunk and made a fool of herself on the dance floor, writhing obscenely with this disgusting senior who had a fake arm. She made him twist it out and up like Robert E. Lee leading his men into battle, then she left him alone like that with his arm in the air in the middle of a song while she went to the ladies' room to throw up.

"The next morning she slept through her first class. She went into town to Marshall Field's and came back with three different brass alarm clocks. Each one cost a hundred dollars."

Good. She was spoiled. She deserved less sympathy.

"What else?" I said.

"Her parents gave a swimming pool to the college in their hometown, and she flew back for fifteen minutes to be present at the dedication."

"What town?"

"Columbia, South Carolina. She was always flying home for a wedding, a funeral, a ball."

"What were her parents like?"

"They were fabulous," Nora said. "We adored them. When they came to school to visit, we all flirted with her dad. He was ten feet tall, it seemed. Gray hair, chiseled features. He was a colonel. We couldn't believe it—he still talked about us Yankees as if the Civil War had just ended. Her mother was ditsy, but she called the shots. They would take a select few of us out to a fancy restaurant.

Instead of inviting people discreetly so no one's feelings would get hurt, they did it publicly so everyone who was slighted would know."

"Did you ever get to go?"

"Always."

"Because you were her friend?"

"No, because of how I stood and how I looked at them when they made their cut."

"How *did* you do it?"

"I looked important. I looked aloof and critical. And I looked rich."

"Where'd you learn that?"

"From her."

❖

"What happened," I asked Boz one fall afternoon, "to estrange you two?"

Boz was looking into my eyes. He lowered his irises a bit and there was the past.

"Something happened on our honeymoon. We never resolved it."

"Where'd you go?"

"Greece."

I envisioned Janice writhing obscenely on the dance floor of a small taverna with a young Zorba while Boz got drunk at the bar. "She *did* something?" I asked.

He blinked. It was still hard to swallow, whatever it was. "That's all I feel like saying."

I waited while he finished remembering things.

"What was the original appeal?" I asked. I expected him to say she got engaged on the rebound. Or his family wanted them to marry to unite two fortunes.

"It was the best time of our lives," he said. Suddenly I was choking with jealousy. "I saved her from an embarrassing situation. Not because I liked her. But because I was there and I could, so I did. She reacted with such beautiful *candor,* I was floored. She was so *real.* And, of course, beautiful. It was like admiring a bouquet—then having it whisper to you."

I waited until my jealousy dissipated to speak again. After all, I *wanted* as my lover the kind of man who would marry a great woman for a great reason.

"Would it be different if you two had children?" I asked.

He flinched. I didn't know that it was a sore subject, that they had tried and failed and blamed each other and tried and failed again. "Family is not all it's cracked up to be," he said.

"That's easy to say," I said. "When you're not an orphan."

His eyes scanned my face with a fearful tentativeness I had not seen before. He was deciding whether or not he wanted to know more.

"Okay, what happened?" he said. I told him. They were simple statements of fact, but I had never spit them out in a row before—to a stranger or a friend. He listened as if he were both, but for days afterward when he saw me entering the cottage door, afloat with love, he looked at me as if I were a car whose specs had changed halfway through the warranty.

One afternoon we skipped the sex and went out in the boat. In the middle of the lake he turned off the motor. We rocked awhile, not saying anything, just looking at the water. "That history you gave me about your family," he said. "It makes me admire you." The shock of the missing approval, coming so late in life, so long after it was needed, injected so benignly in me from someone whose judgment was so objectively sane, made me sick for three days, as if I were getting all my recommended inoculations from ages two to sixteen at once in a single needle.

It got colder. We made love under the blankets. One afternoon we did it with our clothes on. Cottage love was over. I wanted us to rent an apartment somewhere. "But where?" he said. He knew too many people everywhere. We went back to the Cloverleaf.

❖

I was in the darkroom a lot in November, developing and printing the photographs I'd taken of the cannery on the Delaware River for its annual report. I'd forgotten to make plans for Thanksgiving. I'd also forgotten to shop. I took a break and rummaged through the cupboards, looking for Thanksgiving dinner. My menu was fried eggs, sardines, and hash browns. For dessert I had two cigarettes. Then I did what I'd been doing so much more of lately. I got in the car and headed for the cottage. I liked to sit there with the heater on and the motor running, watching the water sparkle. I liked to be near the site of more intimacy than I ever thought I could give or receive.

There was no traffic—everyone else in the world was eating Thanksgiving dinner. I flew south on Highway 6, hooking a left, then a right, veering right again at the fork onto the Boswells' private road. I loved the curves in that road. I always drove them with my spine on fire because they led to Boz—three big esses and I was in his arms.

That night, I forgot the last ess. I drove into a ditch. My forehead hit the windshield, which shattered symmetrically like a spiderweb. The ground tilted forty-five degrees. My headlights burned twin troughs of light into the reeds.

The nearest house was a quarter of a mile away. A nice couple let me in. They sat me down in front of the television with pumpkin pie to watch the Charlie Brown special while they called AAA.

The tow truck came. The driver's name was Toppy. He was taller and heavier than most men, softer and jollier, too, as if a regular-size man, emotions and all, had been inflated. His dark eyebrows rose at the bridge of the nose, and his mouth at rest formed a slack-cutting smile. I sat in the cab beside him as he pulled the Saab out of the ditch. The grille was crunched, the left front wheel bent, the windshield destroyed.

"You'll be out of commission for two weeks or better," he said. As we drove back to town together, I kept looking over my shoulder at the Saab, crumpled and dangling from his big hook. I had an alibi ready. "I was lost," I said. He just nodded. "I was trying to turn around down there," I said.

"It happens," he said.

Toppy's Texaco station was right across from the town house where Boz practiced law. Toppy picked up the phone and called Boz at home to say he'd towed another girl off the family's private road. Her name was "Tammy." Was that all right?

I was confused. Boz asked to speak to me.

"Are you okay?" he said.

I said I was fine.

"Were you—expecting me?" he asked. I said I wasn't. I said I was fine, everything was fine.

Boz asked Toppy to drive me home. Toppy did.

I tried to pay him, but he said it was all taken care of. "Your forehead's still red," he said. "Sure you don't need a hospital or nothing?"

"I'm sure," I said.

I lay in bed wide-awake, rigid with grief. My head felt like a tumor boiling on my neck. It wasn't from hitting the dashboard. It was from the revelation that Boz had met *women* in the cottage. I was not the first. Not the first. It hurt to the quick. It meant there'd be someone after me, too. I lay there competing in my imagination with whoever had been in the cottage with Boz before, wondering what their bodies were like compared with mine, and whether he did to them what he did to me. He did, of course. Whatever they do, men do to everyone.

By midafternoon, all of Dustin knew. A series of unique, medieval splatting sounds slammed the front window of the gallery, all loud enough to bring me out of the darkroom. Fran Mrzoz, the Polish farmer's widow, was winding up like a catapult and hurling mud balls at my window. I was shunned.

❖

What made it hardest was that the car wasn't there. I kept going outside to get into it to get away from everything, but it wasn't there. It was like having arms and legs but no torso—I couldn't run, I couldn't fight. I sat and smoked on the back stoop, looking at the spot where my Saab used to be. I watched the winter wind blow over the swamp where the pond used to be. A scenic green body of water collected briefly there during the spring thaw. By midsummer it was muck; by fall it was nearly dry.

One day a yellow dog came up out of the swamp. It moved toward me so slowly, I thought I was hallucinating. There was a thick pale green film over both its eyes. That and the way it held its head made me understand that it was blind. I put food out, then disappeared inside to watch. It fed.

I had a dog back in Watertown. I always wondered what happened to him the night of the fire. No pets were mentioned in the police report. I prayed that he got away.

Every day, the blind yellow dog came up from the swamp. I put food out, then disappeared. One day I stayed. It ate in front of me, nervously, pausing to listen before swallowing, stopping halfway through the bowl to sniff the air. "Yes, I'm still here," I said. He came to me. He let me pet his ears. He let me comb out his burrs.

Next door the Tuckers' German shepherd was dumbfounded. He stood there on all fours, straining against his short leash, his head cocked, watching this piece of yellow trash that blew up from the Dustin swamp, stinking like crud, receive the love and attention he deserved. For seven years he'd asked for nothing from the Tuckers and all he'd gotten was increased confinement and ever more violent corporal punishment. *I'll be goddamned,* his eyes seemed to say as he watched the yellow dog get love, food, and no leash.

❖

I heard my car, idling with her beloved Swedish accent. I ran out of the darkroom. There she was, new windshield, new wheel, new grille, and Toppy behind the wheel. He started to hurry off—his son was double-parked on the shoulder in their tow truck.

"Toppy," I said. "The cottage—how many *were* there?" I meant girls caught. He knew what I meant.

"Mr. Boswell's been good to me," he said.

"Mr. Boswell's been good to me, too," I said.

"Detering, he don't know about but two," Toppy said to cheer me up, throwing his head west toward the new PO. "You. And that Linda. The kinky one that left sex toys down there and food."

"Food." In my jealous scenarios, I hadn't thought of food.

"Cucumbers, mostly. Everybody got a kick out of that."

I swallowed for a while. "So, how many?" I asked.

He looked at me. "Four."

"Four! Four?"

"It's a bad turn," he said by way of explanation, the way a man would.

I made the call. I got in and drove. I drove to the Cloverleaf and I floored it. I waited for Boz. I made him pay. I made him pay in passion. I made him do things that were new. I needed to leave a mark, a deeper, finer mark on him than anyone who had come before me or would ever come after. I told him this was my intention. I asked him if I succeeded. He said I had.

❖

Now that everyone knew everything, I saw Janice everywhere. At the health food store. At red lights. At the A-1 Dry Cleaners, there was a line. The cashier couldn't find the sports jacket. Janice didn't have the ticket. Leisurely and unapologetically, she repeated, "Herringbone. More black than gray. Forty-eight long." Around and around the chemically scented, plastic-wrapped garments paraded on the oval chrome ceiling track. "Y'all can't have lost it," she said. "You'll break his heart."

Twice the cashier went right past it. "Behind the black dress," I piped up from the back of the line the third time Ted Boswell's herringbone sports jacket rounded the bend. Janice turned and smiled, enjoying what I'd done without caring about me.

❖

The last time I saw her was at the vet. She was there, waiting to have Ted Boswell's gray mare put down. Ted had show horses. Janice liked to ride. That's how the affair got started. It was a Tuesday in the middle of December. I was smoking on the back stoop and petting the yellow dog when the shepherd next door got loose. He ran over to my place and bit off my yellow dog's tail.

The yellow dog watched it happen. He didn't run. He didn't even yelp. His whole life was a string of abuses he thought were uses. He waited in place, holding his head in that special blind way, while the shepherd bounded over to maim him.

I charged into the vet's office with the yellow dog in my arms bleeding all over my leather jacket. I didn't wait my turn. I was too upset. Anyone could see how upset I was, letting a mangy stray bleed like that on a good leather jacket.

I went barging to the head of the line. I yelled at the receptionist, my voice cracking, "Fix my dog *now.*" I felt it, that information in the gut that was tapping me on the shoulder, saying, *Take a look around.* I didn't take a look around. I got in a screaming match with the receptionist, who was Irish with red hair, the kind of person who never loses a screaming match because she knows how they go.

The people standing in line were looking at me—one had a parakeet shivering with the flu, one had a cat with a broken leg, one had a Labrador with wheels for back legs. The people waiting in chairs were looking at me, too—there were more cats, a parrot, a boy with a lamb, and Janice, wearing red lipstick and a gray silk pantsuit. Our eyes met. She considered me in a manner deeply attentive, dispassionately curious, emphatically nonjudgmental.

Everyone else was embarrassed for me. I knew what they were thinking, and it should have humiliated me into shutting up, but I couldn't stop repeating, "Fix *my* dog *now*."

What they all saw was a girl with long yellow hair in a dog-colored leather jacket, in hysterics, holding a bleeding stray who didn't need to be held and who was going to be fine. What they all were thinking was this: *she thinks the dog is her when she was little and hurt and asked for help and no one heard.*

The receptionist was gritting her teeth and speaking superciliously to me. "You *will* be quiet, or you *will* be removed."

Suddenly calm erupted in the waiting room. "Carrie," Janice said. Her soft, southern whiskey voice took its time. It had years to make this point, or any point. The girl with red hair looked over my shoulder with respect and obedience. Her red eyebrows rose, awaiting a command. "Take her dog now."

"Thank you," I said to Janice.

"Thank *you*," she said. For months I didn't know what she meant. She didn't look pregnant yet. She meant that she would be taking Boz back.

❖

We celebrated Christmas in the Cloverleaf. We had only an hour. I was on the way to JFK to fly to L.A. I got there first and plugged in a live miniature Christmas tree that I had decorated with miniature ornaments. I sat primly on the edge of the bed, wearing velvet and lace. He came in with a jumbo carton of baby back ribs and the pearls. They were matching cultured pearls, hand-strung with a platinum clasp. He handed them over in a velvet box. He didn't know how to wrap.

We sat side by side on the bed, eating the ribs. I gave him the sweater he wanted. And the book. We lay down together in our clothes and held each other, looking at the tree until it was time to go.

Something about a close time between a man and a woman makes them think they'll never have to work at it again. I expected our January reunion to pick right up where Christmas had left off. On the plane back to Boz, I couldn't quite remember his face.

When I got home, the yellow dog had disappeared. Henry came over to feed it one day and it was gone. Boz had changed, too. He no longer referred to us in the future tense, and then it got even more complicated.

❖

The last time we met at the Cloverleaf, I brought one of the Leicas he had helped me buy at an auction. Boz wanted to try it on me. It happened without my understanding or full cooperation. Three, maybe four commands from Boz got the unconscious tidal wave rolling. "Open your legs a little more. Good. Move your hand over. Good. Throw your head back. Again. Good."

Slowly I became two people. One obeyed the commands like a pet who has no choice. The other floated above her, watching with no feeling. Boz was happy and excited. He'd been wanting to do this since we first made love. He shot a full roll, then put the camera aside to ravish me.

"Your eyes didn't blink," he told me later that night when he'd taken me back to Dustin and filled a prescription of tranquilizers for me. "I asked you if you were okay. You said you were fine.

Then you walked out of the motel room toward the interstate naked. I brought you back. You did it again. You said you had to go home. I put your clothes on and locked the door. When I was in the shower, you lit a cigarette. You rested it on the nightstand and then watched it burn the lampshade. The smoke detector went off and the manager came running into the room with a fire extinguisher."

"Did we go to a hospital?"

"No. I wanted to take you, but you wouldn't go. You kept hitting my chest and saying if I took you, you'd run away."

We were sitting on the bed side by side as he told me this, staring at that layer of space about six feet away where people contemplate the recent past. He was drinking brandy and I was breathing normally again. "I need therapy," I said.

He tucked me in. He kissed me on the forehead. "I'll always love you," he said.

The Girls

Their custom ranch had a duplicitous look. The tan brick, the beige-speckled roof conveyed an almost sinister normalcy. Behind it, in the middle of a great, blond hayfield, was a horse barn that had been painted purple. Emblazoned across one side in bright yellow, hard-to-read lowercase letters was a single word, *woman-art*. I walked through the hay for my job interview.

Parked in back of the purple barn were a dozen vehicles that appeared to be coincidences of internal combustion—a rusted-out white Pontiac with duct-taped polyethylene for a rear window, an old New York City taxicab painted pink, a green windowless Ford Econoline van that had been sideswiped on both sides. I adjusted my salary expectations accordingly.

Inside, motes of dust danced in the shaft of light from the high square window over the hayloft as Frank Sinatra sang "Strangers in the Night." A great disappointment settled over me: all the workers were elderly women. They were docile-faced and white-haired and they sat, smiling into their piecework, at sewing machines spaced across the barn floor in neat rows. Some machines hummed in short bursts. Others produced longer, steady, machine-gun-like volleys.

I was twenty-nine years old. I liked to be near testosterone in the workplace. Across the barn at the production table was the only available source. A large, strong, even-tempered woman with a gray buzz cut whipped a screwdriver out of the pocket of her white carpenter's overalls. "It turned out so right," she crooned as she pried open a fresh gallon of red ink.

Jobs were scarce in this town. Early on, Boz had wanted very much to help me. He set up this job interview at a silk-screen factory run by two clients of his, Donna and Iris. The word *factory* made me expect some men. I had dressed to please them—tight jeans, lots of beads, and my best slashed T-shirt. I approached the big woman— she looked like a Donna. Her skin was evenly pink and pale, the same pink and pale as a sow's. Her front side was soft and fatty in a general way from the neck to the groin. She hummed along with Frank as she unrolled a bolt of snow-white cotton duck.

Her eyes lit up at my tight jeans. "Vell, vell, vell!" she said. Okay, the German commandant thing. She extended her hand to shake. I expected a killer grip, braced for it, then jumped back a step as she tickled my palm. She laughed—an abbreviated pair of snorts, then settled down to impress me.

"You've seen our pot holders in Macy's," she said. "We . . . *created* . . . the Big Strawberry." The pause on either side of the emphasized word she filled by smoothing her open palms with godlike ease over a globe of air at breast height, as if to help me understand the magnitude of the undertaking. She was nodding at me with an oily, celebrity pride, waiting for some confirming gesture. I tried mimicking her nod. She seemed pleased.

"So, trim a wee sample for Nell?" She cocked her head, smiling with one raised lip like Elvis. I thought she was propositioning me in lesbian code, but a frail woman with gray skin and a trembling chin materialized beside me and was taking my elbow.

Nell led me to an idle sewing machine and sat me down. "I think she likes you," she said. She handed me a quilted, untrimmed white-duck pot holder emblazoned with—I *had* seen the Big Strawberry. It was everywhere. My sister had the whole set, including the towels and the oven mitt. My task was to trim the edge with piping. Nell presented me with a huge commercial-size spool of the stuff. She whispered a hint in my ear, "Form your loop first."

I looked over my shoulder. Donna was pouring red ink onto the screen, pulling her squeegee over the silk, printing big strawberries on pot holders, twelve at a time. "Doo-bee-doo-bee-doo," she sang. All the women in the barn stopped sewing to witness my audition.

I thought I'd go for a show of bravado rather than an actual demonstration of skill. My foot hit the pedal hard and stayed there as I sewed the pot holder to my finger.

Nell blinked. She licked her lips. "Now that has never been done here before," she said. She led me to the bathroom to apply first aid. She clipped the pot holder off my finger. "She docks us for waste," she said, and stuffed it into her bra. She held my finger tight under cold running tap water. I looked down on the crown of her head. She was nearly bald. She patted the little needle holes in my finger dry with a clean towel and squeezed on antibiotic cream. "Hold that," she said as she pressed a tiny folded square of gauze in place. I did. She taped it neatly with strong white adhesive tape.

She whispered in my ear, "We're going to give her this," and handed me one of her own pot holders.

"Va-va-va-voom," Donna said. I was hired.

❖

"It's cherry piiiiiiiink and apple blossom white. . . ." Like the rest of us, Donna's crooners started at nine and finished at five. For me, it was the song equivalent of being sneezed on. On cigarette breaks, I sat out in my Saab with the radio on, listening to classic rock.

One day Nell came over to my car window. The Doors were singing, "Love me two times, I'm going away." I turned the music down. "They want to know where you're from," she said.

"Tell them California," I said.

The next day she came over again. "They want to ask you something else," she said. "You can say no."

In the back of my throat, bile ruined the taste of my cigarette. I had all my lies ready.

"They want to know, can they please brush your hair?"

I joined the women on their afternoon coffee break. They took turns brushing and braiding my hair, standing behind me, marveling, while I sat in a chair, facing away like their twenty-nine-year-old doll. They filled their Styrofoam cups from an institutional-size coffee urn provided by Donna, reimbursing her on the honor system, ten cents for black, twelve cents for milk and sugar. They socialized for fifteen minutes—no more, or Donna began to glower—exchanging what I would have called bad news in tones only slightly more consequential than if they were discussing the weather. Right now it was Luellen whose life was eventful. Her grandson had died of leukemia. She hadn't yet gotten up the gumption to launder his T-shirts and dungarees. He'd lived with her for the past three years while his mother finished a stretch in prison.

Donna worked straight through the breaks. Pranks were her way of contributing to the culture of the workplace. One morning Luellen came in, sat down to sew, and farted. A soft chorus of gentle, vulgar laughter collected in the barn. "I used to be good at this," Luellen said. She worked at perfecting Donna's whoopee cushion. By afternoon she had it down. She would wait for a break in the humming of the machines to cut loose. Soft, paper-thin laughter followed.

This was womanart's busiest season. Donna asked me to stay late to help with the cleanup. She cranked up the Peggy Lee—"Fee-vah that's so hard to bear, you give me fee-vah"—and we stood shoulder to shoulder at the sinks, rhythmically brushing down the silk screens, passing them back and forth under the roaring faucets of scalding water, lining them up, sparkling and immaculate, to dry.

She'd started this business in her Cape May basement ten years ago with fifty dollars in her pocket and had built it into a twenty-man plant with an annual gross of half a million dollars. Iris had been a successful seascape artist then. They left their husbands and began an affair. Occasionally Donna complained. She and Iris split the profit fifty-fifty, but she did all the work. Truth be told, Donna had designed the Big Strawberry, though she gave the credit to Iris. Iris had carved out a no-show job for herself. As the designer, she was to come up with new and ever better fruit designs. For a year now Donna had been promising the Macy's buyer a Big Cherry, a Big Plum, a Big Pear.

"And?" I said.

"Nada," Donna said. Her voice grew grave. "It's just a matter of time before homemakers are going to be sick of the Big Strawberry and demand a new fruit. And that will be a dark day for womanart, my friend. A very dark day."

One day the UPS man delivered Donna a box from Wyoming. "Could you shelve this?" she asked me. I took the box cutter from her desk and slit open the carton. I was up to my elbows in Styrofoam peanuts when I inadvertently fondled the full length of her new special battery-operated Double Dong Dildo. "Try it, you'll like it," she quipped.

I turned it on high and chased her around the barn with both bulbous ends vibrating wildly. She shrieked and ran, her arms raised high, flailing the air.

"Now, is that a new drill?" Elsie asked.

"I haven't had fun like that in years," Donna said, flopping down at her desk to catch her breath.

Iris got jealous. Her province was the ranch house. We were never to bother or interrupt her. We had been told that she needed isolation to *create*. I'd seen her a few times doing shoulder stands in the gazebo. Now she began to sweep through the barn on her way to the woods to sketch, a black notebook tucked under one arm. Iris was pretty, tan, fiftyish. She wore her brown hair pulled straight back in a high, extremely neat ponytail, like a dancer. Her eyes were bitter, her smile a beauty exercise, as if she'd read that a smile creates fewer wrinkles than a frown. She projected violent opposites, warmth and envy, grace and hysteria, insecurity and grandeur, all in the space of a few strides.

When she first saw me sitting on a chair while the women brushed my hair, small involuntary waves of hate issued from her eyes. I was twenty years younger, twenty pounds thinner. My ponytail was blond and twenty pounds heavier. The women greeted her as if she were the pope, saying her name, touching her robe, admiring her makeup. At the root of their emotion was respect for magic: she could draw. Iris wanted all their emotion and tried to prevent them from directing any to me. She skillfully contrived to face them while presenting her back to me—no matter how odd the social configuration that resulted.

She didn't like my doing overtime with Donna, either. We must have looked too complicit, standing there at the sinks with the faucets roaring and the steam billowing around us. She began to show up then, too, elbowing her way between us, wearing her skin-tight Pucci leotard, showing Donna new sketches of fruits-in-progress. Donna could not keep her eyes on the fruits. She looked Iris up and down, her eyes wet with passion, and barked playfully as proof of her love.

One day when I went to work, a 350-pound woman with an acne problem was sitting at my sewing machine. Donna was upset. "You're now working for Iris," she said.

I walked across the hayfield to the ranch house. I let myself in. I waited. Much had been attempted to make the living room distinctive. The coffee table was a slab of glass uncomfortably balanced on some kind of plow attachment. Leather hassocks draped with afghans surrounded the table. Half-burnt candles and dusty seashells decorated the available surfaces. Bad oils of the sea crowded the walls. They were all the same—plodding and predictable with an agitated foreground emphasis on reeds.

In an hour Iris appeared, preceded by the tinkle of bracelets as she walked up the long hall from the bedroom wing. She was wearing full makeup and an exercise suit. I counted for her as she did jumping jacks, bicycles, and sit-ups. Next we meditated—she said I wasn't doing it right. Then I made lunch—I didn't do that right, either. After lunch she talked on the phone. I held the nail polish bottle while she did her nails. We looked for the checkbook, then we looked for stamps. I paid three bills.

The next day Iris had a migraine. We withdrew to their purple bedroom, closed the door, drew the draperies, turned the air conditioner on high. Iris ordered me to keep her dosed to the limit with pain medication. I brought her tea, then ice water, then juice. I sat beside her until nightfall, when she sent me away. Their room made me claustrophobic. The sight of their intimate things—two hairbrushes filled with female hair, two nighties on two hooks, two filthy cities of beauty products on the makeup table—nauseated me.

To anchor myself, I memorized a love poem called "She," taped to the wall on Iris's side of the bed. *She moves as water moves, and comes to me, / Stayed by what was, and pulled by what would be.* Now I was jealous. If these two women could find love in spite of their incredibly annoying personality flaws, why couldn't a cute young heterosexual like me?

The migraine went on all week. I followed my instructions precisely and thoroughly, yet Iris was critical and mean. I started popping tranquilizers in the car on the way to work. I missed the barn, the smell of the ink, the humming of the machines, the lives of the women. I even missed the piped-in schmaltz. I could hear it on my cigarette breaks.

Friday, Donna had to go to New York. It was always confusing to see Donna dressed like a woman in a navy suit, gold earrings, and navy heels, leaving her truck behind and driving away in a light blue sedan. Iris asked me for her pills. I looked in the bathroom, in both nightstands, on the bureau, in the kitchen. No pills. Donna had filled the prescription, then inadvertently taken it to New York in her purse. Iris begged me to give her anything that was left in the medicine chest, to kill her if necessary. I ran outside, jumped in my Saab, and drove down Route 23 all the way to Mahwah, where I found and flagged down Donna. When I got back, Iris's eyes were lined with pain, pain, pain. I dosed her and stayed there by her side.

It was after nine when Donna got back. She rewarded me with an extra twenty bucks and a secret: Iris had once attempted suicide. Ahh, suicide. I kept my mother's to myself—along with her homicides. I walked out to my car and sat in the dark for a while, looking at the stern summer stars, clawing the skin on my forearms until they bled.

I hoped my heroic efforts would make Iris trust me, but she remembered nothing of what was done or said. To get through the next week, I took pills. Here it was again, the self-destructive selflessness I grew up specializing in.

I showed up for work on Monday and the door to the ranch house was locked. In the barn Donna gave me a check and said my services were no longer needed. They had expected me to quit, they wanted me to quit, but I didn't know how to. Nell followed me out to the car. "Don't take it personal," she said.

❖

Nell had a stroke. She lost the use of her left arm and hand. Donna called me up at Nell's request to invite me to the retirement party. I went early to help. It was a beautiful summer day. The sky was blue. The sun was warm. Walking through the rolling hay to the purple barn, I felt light on my feet and happy. Boz was helping me find a place to live. We weren't yet lovers, but I would drop by his office at the end of the day to tell him about the ugly real estate listings I'd seen. It was fun, making him laugh. I would miss his company when I no longer needed his daily help.

Around the coffee urn, Elsie fanned out pretty flowered paper napkins and matching plates. I brewed fresh decaf. We tied balloons to Nell's sewing machine. There was a beautiful big sheet cake designed by Iris. A needle and thread made out of frosting seemed to stitch the words *Farewell, Nell.* Iris was on hand to slice and serve. The women gave Nell little gifts they'd sewn or crocheted—doilies, pincushions, sachets. She opened each one graciously, praising it all the while. The spirited way she picked up her dead left hand, made it do something, then tossed it back into her lap without wasting anyone's time made it seem as if we were the ones who'd suffered the setback, not Nell. The women cleaned up the mess, then dragged their chairs into rows under the old hayloft. "What's happening now?" I asked.

"We do this on special occasions," Nell said. "You'll enjoy this."

"Ready?" Iris called up into the loft. Only then did I realize that all this time Donna had been missing from the festivities. Iris cued up a CD. She pushed PLAY. A great orchestral swell filled the barn, maudlin with Neapolitan strings. A mandolin began to plink. Down the ladder from the loft climbed Donna, dressed in a gangstery double-breasted jacket, her short hair blackened with shoe polish.

"When-a the moon hits-a your eye like a big pizza pie, that's a-mor-ay," the voice of Dean Martin sang. Donna lip-synched, miming him perfectly: the idiosyncratic Italian head wags she had down pat; her half-closed eyes were drunk with that special Mediterranean strain of maternally induced macho self-love. She strutted, she strolled, she was by turns oily and sincere. "Bells will ring, ting-a-ling-a-ling, ting-a-ling-a-ling and you'll sing, 'Vita bella' . . ."

The faces of the womanart girls were sober and rapt, reflecting the importance of being offered live entertainment. Nell whispered in my ear, "She's not really singing."

Over in the wings, Iris seemed pleased with her breasts, gazing down at them, admiring the way they matched, tucking the tail of her polyester blouse in more tightly in back to increase the effect. "Hearts will play, tippy-tippy-tay, tippy-tippy-tay like a gay tarantella . . ."

I was smiling stupidly. I couldn't help wagging my head to the music, tapping my foot in time. I felt tacky and bawdy. No need to wait for love until my personal problems were solved. I could go now to the man who was willing to help me in so many little ways—and let him help me a lot.

Shirley Girt of Girt Real Estate

She was a little too old to dye her hair so even an auburn or to wear the girlish clothing she favored. Her yellow sundress was starched to the limit, which only served to emphasize the soft, wrinkled, aging shoulders beneath the straps. She carried a large white purse with a loud clasp and drove a loud white Oldsmobile, which she floored at the slightest provocation, sometimes, I began to suspect, simply because her large right foot twitched. Her eyes were shiny, round, and flat; they looked sewn to her soft, white face like buttons.

I sat before Shirley Girt of Girt Real Estate with my hair in a recently tangled swirl about my shoulders, wearing a stolen blue sheath and smelling faintly of aftershave from the nape of my neck to the hollows of my knees. To Shirley, it was the scent of art. It was as if she knew my future before I did.

I was not a trusting person then, yet I put my trust in Shirley Girt. She was like the old, soft plain doll I had superstitiously loved the most in childhood, assuming the ice-cold, beautiful dolls

arranged so rigidly on my pillow could not or would not love me back.

I asked to see rentals. Shirley flicked through the listing book, making small noises of discovery—bargain noises, they might have been called. "This should be fun," she said as we both listened to the printer printing out listing sheets. She saved her disclaimer for the Olds, saying as we drove, "Some of these I haven't seen."

She hooked a left at a DEAD END sign and drove to the dead part. "This is for rent," she said. It was a long, low dairy barn built of cinder blocks, with three small evenly spaced windows on each side and a ventilator on the roof. We got out of the car. I followed her into the dank, echoing building.

"These would have to come out," she said, wrestling with a stanchion with a concrete base where a cow was once milked. There were fifty-nine more just like it. I was speechless.

"No?" she said, helping me out.

We drove to New Jersey to examine a two-room cabin with nesting red squirrels and no plumbing. Across the Delaware River back in New York, we inspected an abandoned eighteen-unit motel. Closer to home, we toured a duplex half-finished by a genius of the half-finish—half a floor, half a wall, half a roof. Shirley talked up each rental with astounding neutrality, itemizing the selling points in measured, newsy tones in spite of my obvious horror, until I stopped her—and she stopped on a dime.

"Do you have your calendar with you?" she asked, whisking out hers at the end of the day. The sheer potential she'd exposed me to had refreshed and rejuvenated her. I had no calendar. I had no strength. I could have run a small galaxy with the creative energy I had expended, dredging up a workable enthusiasm for each unacceptable listing, discarding it well beyond the unthinkable

stage, long after I'd warped my brain in the effort to forge a new identity to match the rental.

"Any day is good," I said.

I wore my own jeans the next time I went out with Shirley. I wore my Nikon, too. I needed to anchor myself in reality so my reaction time would be quicker. It seemed to work—the properties we looked at were lovely. I went floating from room to room, dreaming of a graceful life amid *imported bath tile with whirlpool overlooking small stream* while Shirley happily examined the private incriminating trove of medications lining the medicine cabinet or read the owner's personal papers stored inside a closed Chippendale. Once, with no qualms whatsoever, she carried an antique wrought-iron shelf out to her car and put it in the trunk. "What a shame to throw this out," she said. "Can you believe it was in the garbage?" I wasn't so sure that it was.

Each time I asked Shirley the monthly rent of a property, she named an amount that broke my budget by a factor of ten. It seemed odd that not one of the owners was home. Looking back, I realized these high-end, luxury domiciles weren't for rent at all—they were second homes and were for sale. My tour with Shirley counted as a showing.

"Dustin is *the* up-and-coming arts town," Shirley said our third time out. The Olds rolled to a stop. It didn't look like a town. It looked like an accidental intersection of two roads that led emphatically somewhere else. The fronts of some buildings faced the sides and backs of others. It looked unprepared and undressed, as if it were permanently surprised from behind. There was nowhere to turn for privacy. The rust-colored antiques store was closed and apparently had been for decades. NO LUNCH read a hand-lettered sign in the window of the yellow luncheonette. Across the high-

way, a defiant green house bent toward the road, bearing up under twin bell curves of road dust, a high parabola for trucks, a lower one for cars. It appeared to be rebuffed by the ugly, multifamily building across the road: KEEP OUT, PRIVATE PROPERTY, KEEP OUT read the signs along the fence.

"First, the arts tour," she said. She drove up Highway 6, pointed at a big white house, and said, "This is a very artistic woman."

She drove back down the highway, through the crossroads, past the ice cream stand that had become the Shurberrys' insurance agency, and halfway into a cul-de-sac, at the end of which was a dark red bungalow. "She makes crafts at Christmastime," Shirley said.

"Which crafts?" I asked.

"Centerpieces. She has all the Styrofoam balls and cubes. She has every color of ribbon, every color of sequin, every color candle. I'm not handy myself."

Shirley backed out of the cul-de-sac, swung a left, then a right. We drove up a hill to a native stone Arts and Crafts bungalow nestled in a meadow overlooking miles of rolling fields. "Saving the best for last," she said. "This is the Doctor." The house made a face at us, the stone steps gritting like bared teeth, the windows on either side of the door as blank as eye sockets in a skull, the veranda shading the front elevation like a single swarthy eyebrow.

We drove back down the hill to the crossroads. "This is mine," Shirley said, parking the Olds in front of the feed store. Looking back, I was sold the very second I saw the word FEED, high and historic, right where I needed it to be, in fading capitals, along the storefront's turn-of-the-century ziggurat facade. The siding was bleached gray by time and weather.

Inside, the store was long and narrow, high and dim, with pressed tin ceilings and wide-plank oak floors. The fixtures were gone, but I could still smell the clean, condensed-nutrient smell of grain dust. I walked the length of the floor twice. I could feel my fate coming to meet me.

In the rear of the store there was a little room curtained off with a bit of worn tapestry sagging from a rope. Here the former owner had lived, Shirley said, without adding *and died*. I was emotionally drawn to his little white cot, his little white stove, though Shirley Girt literally pulled me in the opposite direction.

"All new!" she said, opening the hollow-core door to the bathroom. She meant *used*. There was a rusting metal stall shower, a dented Masonite vanity, a half-silvered mirror. The toilet was green and it cringed in place, held hostage by jumpy, discount red plaid wallpaper.

"I did it myself," Shirley said. I offered her the only disappointment of our long acquaintance by showing no measure of surprise. She presented a lease. My signature wobbled with joy on the line.

"Now for a treat!" she said.

Back in the Olds, she floored it, driving north up Highway 6 to a field filled with old white bathtubs. JOHN THE JUNKOMOLOGIST read the ragged painted plywood sandwich board in the ditch. Shirley drove through the tubs, which took some doing—they were lying about in high grass in a chaotic pattern, as if dropped there by a Red Cross plane. There were sinks, stoves, and refrigerators. A flock of chickens waddled about, clucking and pecking, competing for invisible things in the dirt that fascinated them, shitting in the sinks.

Shirley parked beside a barn painted entirely with words:

SERIOUSLY

HELLO. I'M "JOHN THE JUNKOMOLOGIST."
35 MM PROJECTOR. CHILDRENS USED BIKE. CUSTOM
WOODWORKING.
ODDS AND ENDS. COMPLETE PRINTING AGENT.
CARDS & STATIONERY. FREE GIFT WHEN YOU BUY.
NO CHECKS. NOT RESPONSIBLE FOR ACCIDENT.
GOD BLESS THE U.S.A. SMILE.

"They have everything here," Shirley said.

John himself sat near the door in a lawn chair, legs crossed daintily at the knee, reading pornography. He was a fifty-plus man with uncombed hair and half-inch-thick glasses. His mother, an old woman with two shiny warts, one just to the side of her mouth, the other along the jaw, stayed in place behind the cash register.

Wares on display included irregular U.S. Army–issue long underwear, new stainless-steel shoehorns, 100% linen handkerchiefs, paper towels, coasters from the 1950s, used garden tools on special at fifty cents each. Shirley and I both bought shovels. After we paid, John's mother followed me out to the Olds. She got up close to me, her warts almost touching my face. "Would you marry my son?" she said.

"No, she won't," Shirley said. In the Olds she winked, saying, "Welcome to Dustin."

The feed store had become an art gallery with two unsuccessful shows behind it when Shirley Girt began to send me photography customers. In addition to the cannery in Pennsylvania that had hired me to shoot the assembly line for its annual report, the Wickley Chamber of Commerce invited me to do a formal portrait of its new president. He was also president of the Minisink County Trust Company and paid me to photograph his seven branches for an ad campaign. I was in business.

That fall a rumor began to circulate throughout Dustin: Tom and Jean Jaeger were thinking of giving up farming. There was a lot of discussion in the hamlet about what should be done with the Jaegers' six hundred acres on the hill west of Dustin. A school, a nature preserve, a baseball diamond—those were the three uses that people fought about. A couple of times I thought I saw Shirley's white Olds parked at the Jaegers' farmhouse. Before anyone knew it, a deal was struck with a developer from New Jersey. A surveyor came. Next, a flatbed trailer carried a backhoe up the hill. The excavator began to dig the foundations for eight town houses. There were plans for ninety-six more.

The Doctor's handsome native stone house went on the market. Realtors from several counties had prospectives lined up to see it, but the house went quickly to Dave and Ray, two middle-aged guys from Manhattan. They planned to transform it into a French restaurant, Do-Ray-Mi. I thought I saw a white Olds parked behind their black BMW.

By summer there were eight new middle-class families planting petunias and installing swing sets in the town houses on the hill. A steady stream of house hunters toured the model home. The French restaurant fed them lunch.

Then came the blow from which Dustin's three Presbyterians were not to recover. Their church was sold by special arrangement with the synod. A sports outfitter took out the pews and filled up the church with red and green Mad River canoes. Delaware River canoe trips were big business now. I saw the white Olds.

A couple from Connecticut came canoeing and fell in love with the hamlet. They bought the old Dustin Hotel. Down came the ugly fence with its rude KEEP OUT signs. Out went the cheap partitions that broke up the building into welfare apartments. In went a grand central staircase with a solid oak balustrade. Dustin got a bed-and-breakfast.

A year later there were ten of us on Shirley Girt's arts tour. My gallery was number one, though I narrowly beat out John the Junkomologist. New Yorkers were as taken with John's colorful white trashiness as with the odd bargains he had for sale. Plus, every woman between sixteen and sixty got a kick out of the offer of marriage from John's mother.

Soon enough, Shirley Girt put my gallery on the market at a price that reflected the increase in value directly resulting from renovations completed and financed by me. With a loan from my sister, I had to outbid two wealthy women artists from New York City to keep my home and livelihood. In effect, I paid twice to restore it.

As the three of them predatorily stalked the gallery in its gleaming, welcoming, pristine state, eyes twitching with dollar signs, purses itching with checks that were easy to write and quick to bind, there was no trace of the ugly doll. Shirley Girt looked like one of them: tough, sophisticated, and greedy, draped in overly thought-out apparel, clanging with heavy, original, artisanal jewelry, and generally exhibiting a self-interest so amoral, thorough, and chilling as to be indistinguishable from the forces of nature.

Eleanor

"Oh, I dabble—I dabble," Viola said. "But you must meet Eleanor. Eleanor is our resident artist."

I was applying a coat of white paint to the walls of the feed store. The air was hot and still. I had the door open so the paint would dry faster. Viola nearly filled the door. Ever since she had found out I was opening an art gallery across the highway from her luncheonette, she had started wearing big arty jewelry over her sleeveless nylon tops.

"Eleanor did a sketch of a cherry tree in bloom which received a lot of attention in our adult education class," Viola said. Her voice was actually snooty. "You missed a spot." I pushed the roller back and forth over a bluish stain, but it bled through. "Given half a chance, Eleanor could be famous," Viola said arrogantly, almost blamefully. "With you in town, Tamara, it's very likely, wouldn't you say?"

"It's not that simple," I said with authority, though I was just guessing. My life was all new to me. I would have to be more selective about the half-truths I told Viola. She had wanted to know what I was doing here. I had attributed to myself an ideal, a desire to promote little-known artists in a little-known setting, where art was needed most.

"Well, is it possible?" Viola whined. She hung there in the doorway like a giant Kewpie doll, ready to be taken home by the first paying customer. My arm was tired. I cradled the roller in the paint tray.

"It's possible," I said.

Twice during the next couple of weeks, when I went into the luncheonette for a newspaper, I had just missed Eleanor. "She was just here," Viola would say. "I told her all about you. She wants to meet you."

"Good," I said both times. "I'd like to meet her."

Five of the six people who came to my first opening in September, a show of clay masks with American Indian motifs by a guy named Anton from New Jersey, came because they thought the gallery was the annex to the Odds 'N Ends antiques store next door. Viola was the exception.

"Eleanor wanted to come, too," she said. "But she's so busy with the farm. And the children—she's got the eight. I have to keep reminding her that art should come first."

"Good," I said. "It should."

We repeated ourselves in October. I was showcasing plywood-and-straw constructions by a German woman, a sculptor from Woodstock. A few of her artist friends came, rounding out the names in the guest book to an even eight. Viola, once again, was the only local in attendance. She heard me agree to review the slides of two artists for future shows. "Oh, you should give Eleanor a show!" she cried.

"Viola," I said, careful to avoid a sarcastic tone, "I've never seen her sketches. I've never seen *her*."

Viola's face collapsed for a moment. "I will get that sketch to you," she said. "With or without Eleanor."

It was November—and cold—the day Viola left the luncheonette unattended long enough to run across County Route 1, throw open the studio door, and shout, "Tamara, we're set. Saturday. Eleanor's free!"

Henry was in the gallery, warming up with a cup of coffee. He had a knack for appearing soon after I had brewed fresh coffee, made myself a sandwich, or opened a box of doughnuts. "Bet you I know why Eleanor's free," he said.

"Why?"

"Hunting season. Her husband's hunting."

"So?"

"He don't like her to go nowheres unless he goes somewheres. He wants her car *in the driveway* when he gets there. You should see them sometimes, trying to beat each other home!" He laughed with glee, as if by being a bachelor, he was getting away with something: he never had to bother laying down the law to a woman. He was an innocent man, and yet what he described left a cold, clamping sensation in the pit of my stomach, the same sensation I felt when I saw my parents' life insurance policies side by side— Mutual of Omaha gave Nora and me $75,000 for Dad, $25,000 for Mom.

Early Saturday afternoon, Viola brought Eleanor to the studio with her sketch. Eleanor wore a man's old khaki parka over a man's plaid flannel shirt. She was on the tall side and too thin, her eyes deeply sunken in their sockets. "Show Tamara your garnet," Viola instructed.

"Oh!" Eleanor flashed a wide, spooky smile that seemed to me to be a dangerous waste of energy, given her pallor. She reached beneath her shirt and pulled out a thin gold teardrop on a chain. A garnet filled the curve of the drop. "It's different," Eleanor offered.

"It's beautiful," I said. "Did your husband give it to you?"

Viola howled—a lengthy physiological event, her bust and stomach clapping together in great wallops while she helplessly surveyed the ceiling.

"No, I don't think so," Eleanor said.

"I gave it to her," Viola said, wiping her eyes. "Last year."

"For my thirty-third birthday," Eleanor said. She looked fifty.

The sketch of the tree was done in pen and ink, mounted and framed by Eleanor with a wide pale blue mat. The whole thing was wrapped in saran. I held it at arm's length and looked at it for quite a while. Eleanor joined me. She seemed to marvel at her own work, the way a woman would marvel at her sleeping child. It was very, very good. There was something sprightly in the technique that gave the tree life. I told her so.

Eleanor responded with a long rehearsed description of which bough she had drawn first and which rock she had sat on to draw it, and so on through the entire drawing. Her dentures clicked against the roof of her mouth as she talked. I told her to bring in the rest of her work. Her face came to a complete halt.

"This is the only one she has matted," Viola explained.

"That doesn't matter," I said. "I don't need a mat to appreciate what I'm looking at." Eleanor seemed unrelieved.

I offered them coffee. They hemmed and hawed and then, when they coaxed it out of me, I amended the offer to include white wine. We drank a bottle and a half together. Viola led a discussion, largely bitter, about men, which ended when I told them what I looked for in a man. "Openness and honesty," I said with the authority that came so easily to me in their company.

Eleanor looked at me as if I'd said, "Three penises." And the fact that I had experienced these virtues secretly, in units of one hour several times a week, should have disqualified them as my contribution to the discussion.

We closed by agreeing that we three should do this again soon, but from then on, whenever Eleanor's brown Chevy station wagon passed the gallery, it contained anywhere from five to nine silhouettes and was heading home at high speed. Very often, a silver truck chugged by in her wake.

For January, I was planning a group show featuring local landscapes by local artists. Viola talked proprietarily about where Eleanor's work would go—she staked out the best wall. She pouted when I reminded her that I had still seen only one sketch.

The holidays came, which is when I flew to L.A. to visit my sister. I kept postponing my return flight—I was punishing Boz. I wasn't about to sit around in the room behind my gallery, waiting for a fast, hushed phone call from Wickley while round after round of wealthy in-laws, healthy, living family members, and lifelong friends filed through his wreath-covered door.

Within an hour of my return, Viola appeared at my back door. She was wearing the new black beret and the woven poncho she got for Christmas. "Eleanor's never going to bring the rest of her sketches in," she said. "If you want to see them, you're going to have to go over there."

We went together. She lived in a tenant farmhouse that hadn't been painted in forty years. The front stoop was a stack of cinder blocks. She met us at the door. She'd gotten thinner; the hollow light in her eyes had gotten hollower. There were nine empty

hooks on the living-room wall with nine pairs of galoshes underneath. On the tenth hook was Eleanor's khaki parka. The floor
was covered with linoleum. Something smelled of manure. "This
is my office," Eleanor said, sweeping us over to an old steel file cabinet that had been painted a fifties powder blue.

"Show Tamara the sketch of the lean-to in the onion field,"
Viola said.

Eleanor pulled out a drawer and thumbed through the files.
"Let's see," she kept saying. "Lean-to. Lean-to." All she came up
with were farm bills. She tried another drawer. I looked out the
picture window. The metal mailbox, also painted blue, leaned
away from the road on its post, as if it were shrinking from contact. Eleanor disappeared from the living room. When she returned, she had a violin under her chin and was playing it.

"Stop, please, Eleanor," Viola said. Eventually we just left. To
me, she said, "The holidays were hard on her."

The advance publicity went well. A reporter from the *Wickley
Citizen* brought a photographer out to the gallery. I found myself
pointing them toward the cherry tree. Eleanor's art was on the
front page.

"This could make all the difference," Viola said, mooning over
the newspaper picture. "For Eleanor, this could mean *ev-ry-thing.*"
She gave the word all her teeth, both lips, and the full athletic
reach of her tongue.

I called Eleanor to see how she felt about it. "Yee-gads," she
kept saying, as if she were the center of a scandal.

On Sunday afternoon, an hour before the opening began,
Eleanor parked her brown Chevy wagon across the highway, fac-
ing home. She was wearing an out-of-date pink suit, probably an
Easter outfit. She looked uncomfortable in her high heels.

"Come and look around," I said as she entered, but she seemed intimidated by the expanse of polished oak floor. She pulled a chair up to the big display window by the door, slipped off her shoes, and sat down with her eyes on the highway. I uncorked the wine, laid out the crackers and cheese. Henry came in from next door as if on cue.

"Congratulations," he said to Eleanor. "You're famous!" She winced. He chewed awhile. "Where's Marty at?"

"Down to Hapsburg," she said. She cast her eyes south. "Looking at a used harvester."

There was a lull. Henry chewed, Eleanor watched the road, I loaded my Nikon. Then everything happened at once. Cars rolled into Dustin and parked along both shoulders of the highway, constricting traffic to a single lane. The phone started ringing with calls from people who were lost. I was giving directions to one such caller when I heard Eleanor say, "Yee-gads!" She stabbed her feet into her heels and ran out the front door before I could photograph her in front of her picture.

Come back, Eleanor, I want to say every time I think of her ducking and losing and fleeing her art. She was even better at it than I was. Her husband's silver truck was stuck so long in gallery traffic that before it chugged past the window toward home, three different ladies had time to scrutinize the oils, acrylics, and watercolors and remark to me their special interest in buying the cherry tree.

I didn't laugh, he laughed for me a little too long. leave when I asked him to, so I left. I went next doo. store.

"Boy, does he rake it in," Henry said as we watched Da away.

"What does he do?"

"He's the artificial inseminator."

I could just see Dave L. Garson with his arm shoulder-deep in a cow—for a little too long. I watched Henry's face, expecting the eyes to crinkle up in fun, but they didn't, so I had to laugh alone, which always bothered him. He was afraid I was laughing at him. "What's so funny?" he asked.

"It seems like a perverted profession to me," I said.

"Oh no," Henry said. "He gets calls from five counties."

That evening when I was sautéing onions and chopping up a green pepper for my supper, there was a knock. No one had ever come to the back door when it was dark except Boz. I ran to open it. Dave L. Garson stepped in and closed the door behind him— his tan truck was idling in my driveway, blocking my Saab. He was selling raffle tickets, he said, which reminded him of a story that turned into a dirty joke. His voice was too loud for just us, his movements were jerky, and somehow in the course of the telling, he craftily seated himself at the kitchen table. I was surprised and off-balance and I fell into the trap of believing a polite response would get rid of him sooner.

I said I was busy right then, I didn't have time to consider raffle tickets or to visit. He looked around the room and commented idly on a few of my photographs, then asked me what kind of things I did in the big double bed to make it so messy and rumpled. At that point, I felt scared. I moved toward the door. I thought I'd

Dave L. Garson & His Wife, Flo

None of the thirty-nine residents of Dustin, New York, knew about Boz that first summer. They would, soon enough, thanks to my little Saab mishap. But during those long, hot, languid afternoons at the Cloverleaf Motel, we were still a secret.

His caseload got heavier as August turned to September, so each time we met I expected him to announce that we'd have to stop for a while, maybe even for good. Instead, as the nights got cooler and the air crisper and the leaves of the maple tree on the crossroads turned slowly to flame, so did Boz. He wanted more, not less.

One time he couldn't wait for our next arranged motel meeting, and risked coming to the feed store after midnight. Compared with his spacious, antiques-filled Tudor in Wickley, my place was nothing, one room behind the art gallery or photo studio or whatever it was—I was still trying different things. Whatever it was, he liked it and we both slept well, so well we slept through the 2:00 A.M. alarm. I woke by chance at 4:35 and got him safely back to

Wickley before anyone who might recognize his red Mercury was up and about.

He started coming over regularly, and one of those nights we had time for a quick little breakfast. As we sat in my bed, eating scrambled eggs and toast with raspberry jam and drinking brandy, we decided it was perverse that we'd never eaten a meal out together. He made a dinner reservation at an old Italian villa on the Jersey side of Wickley Mountain, selecting an evening when he was supposed to attend the County Bar Association meeting. I felt important. I felt legitimate.

I closed early that day—closing an art gallery in the middle of nowhere was, of course, a mere formality, locking the door and turning out the light. Back in my room, I turned the radio on, drew the curtain, and dressed in all of Boz's favorite things: the high, black boots, the black turtleneck, the black leather miniskirt, the earrings from India, a jangle with heavy silver bells. I tied two feathers into my hair at the side, then took them out—I'd gone too far. I had just dabbed jasmine essential oil behind each ear, where Boz would go looking for it soon after his first taste of wine, when the gallery doorbell rang—two polite, brief rings, echoing against the oak floor like little question marks.

I was reluctant to answer. I didn't want my romantic mood disturbed. I didn't want any locals seeing me in my Boz getup. I didn't want to be late. I had good directions, but I didn't know the roads. And yet, perhaps because I'd never heard that particular ring before, I went ahead and answered the door.

The caller was standing squarely, undemandingly in front of the display window, looking in, the way birds look in. The pockets of her tired yellow cardigan drooped in front like old breasts. She was holding a can with a coin slot on top. I opened the door.

She identified herself, though I didn't catch the name. She was collecting for multiple sclerosis; she was area chairman of the annual drive. She would be happy to come back some other time if I was closed. "No, please come in," I said. "I want to contribute."

Her sister had died of MS in March, she said, though it had taken her nineteen years to die. "Once that happens, you want to do something," she said. "No matter how small." I got out the checkbook. I wanted to do more than fish around the bottom of my purse for some quarters.

She looked at the wood-and-straw sculptures on display. She asked a few intelligent questions about them. She said she was proud of the image I was bringing to Dustin with the art and all. She said she tacked the announcement of my show on the bulletin board of the hospital in Wickley where she worked part-time as a nurse. She warned me not to give up—it took a long time to be accepted in this town, she said. She and Dave had lived here ten years and some people still treated them like newcomers. *Dave?*

I looked hard at the back of her as she moved on to the next sculpture—this was Dave L. Garson's wife. I sat there, pen poised over the blank dollar-sign line, feeling vaguely corrupt. Her husband had accosted me my first week in Dustin, coming up behind me in the Agway and knocking a handful of nails out of my hand. He followed me back to the gallery, blocking the window with his big tan truck with DAVE L. GARSON painted on the door.

He was built like a wooden clothespin, tall and all legs with a small head. He always wore the same thing, a gray jumpsuit with DAVE L. GARSON embroidered on the back. He had a baby face, the kind women think is cute and men want to punch; he wore a baseball cap pulled down low on the forehead. He told a few jokes that were a little too dirty in a voice that was a little too loud, and when

walk down to Hale's Sunoco. Hale was open and he liked me; his son was going to build me a darkroom. Dave L. Garson stood up, physically blocking my exit but continuing his maddeningly innocuous, socially acceptable patter. His technique produced confusion, guilt, and fear.

I picked up the telephone and, without thinking about it, called Boz at home—the forbidden number. The pause before the first ring seemed unusually long, the ring itself even longer. Dave L. Garson had not advanced—he was still talking, lurking by the door.

The receiver lifted on Boz's end. I could hear laughter from a television show. "Hello?" It was Janice. I wanted nothing more than to eliminate her. I knew Boz was right there. More laughter—they were watching a sitcom. I disconnected the call and stood there shaking for a second, smelling the onions as they slowly burned black.

"Leave now," I said.

He stayed. I dialed O. "Operator," I said though the line was still ringing, "get me the police."

"I'll tell them you're a cockteaser," he said. He opened the door. "They'll believe me, not you." He left.

I turned off the range and drove to Wickley. There was a booth in the Co-See Coffee Shop that I liked. I ordered my usual omelette and fries and thought the sight of Boz's television antenna rising up behind the drugstore would make me feel closer to him. It didn't; it made me feel farther away.

Now, with Dave L. Garson's wife standing there in front of me, I wondered if Flo, as she urged me to call her, knew about her husband's behavior. Everyone else did. Dave made the rounds. I lowered pen to paper and filled in the amount of the check for double what I ordinarily would have given. Surely everyone else did, too. Flo must have noticed how easily her can was filled compared with the other MS volunteers.

Flo thanked me—her expression was so innocent, so effortlessly *good,* that it stayed with me all the way down Highway 6. I started to feel very much in the wrong about Boz and me. I thought about the afternoon in the Cloverleaf Motel when I had told Boz the whole Dave L. Garson story. Boz punched the wall with his fist, swearing he would put Dave L. Garson out of business one way or another. I thought this was funny—I kept picturing that arm of Dave's—but Boz got even angrier at me for laughing. I was the one who was harassed. I was the one who was unprotected. Shouldn't I be the angry one? Shouldn't Flo? I realized then that like sex, harassment isn't just something between a man and a woman; it's also something between the man and other men.

At some point after the intersection with Route 23, on my way to the restaurant, I missed the left turn that Boz had described as "half a mile past the rug warehouse." The next guidepost, an animal clinic, did not appear, though I drove for ten miles.

The sun was setting by the time I found a gas station where I could ask directions back to the mountain. I would be an hour late. It all seemed forced. Hiding our love, sneaking around, driving to a deserted mountain to share a meal. One wrong turn and a third of our time alone was gone. And isn't it always, in cases like ours, just a matter of time before the wife finds out? And then it's over. I felt clear: this was as good a night as any to try to say good-bye.

The sign for the restaurant, a large pink arrow, appeared suddenly. I turned in time. My headlights grazed the side of the red Mercury. In that momentary flash of color, my intelligent perspective of the moment before went scattering into the cracks and crevices like so many disgusting bugs at the flick of a light. Just knowing that Boz was seconds away sent my pulse racing, my spine arching. I left the Saab parked at a reckless angle and went rushing blindly through the dark, not stopping to search the gravel when I heard the soft telltale jangle of an earring fall behind.

Vinnie and Dolly in Jersey

Vinnie's Villa was a pink, Mediterranean-style stucco monstrosity, rife with leaning arches and unstable wrought-iron balconies. Huge flakes of pink paint peeled from the facade. A pair of gleaming black Cadillacs were nosed up to the dry pink fountain as if to nurse. CLOSED TUESDAY read the sign by the door. It was Tuesday. I tried the knob.

The door didn't give. There was a bell off to the side, painted over with pink. I pushed—no sound. I knocked; then when no one came, I pounded with a fist. The door swung open. Vinnie, a man with a sallow, destroyed countenance, bowed to me. His shoulders were broad, his tuxedo dusty.

"Welcome, mademoiselle," Vinnie said in a soft, abused voice. He invited me inside.

Boz was standing right there, looking very much like someone else's husband except that his eyes were wild with potential grief. When he saw me, he took me in his arms, his eyes closed tight, his cheek on my cheek. I knew what he was thinking. A carload of drunken teenagers had driven off this road into the lake on Labor Day and drowned.

"Dolly, she'll be right with you," Vinnie said. He walked to the foot of a spiral staircase. A velvet rope was looped across the steps, preventing access. In rough Italian, Vinnie called up the stairs. Dolly appeared. She was statuesque in her soiled black velvet gown. Her beautiful face was distracted, her pile of peroxide hair slightly askew, as if she had just been molested. Vinnie unhooked the chain. He bowed to us the Italian way, a slinky upper torso innuendo with half-closed eyes, then retreated into a back room, locking the door.

Dolly descended. "Window table or alcove?" she asked flatly, her eyes focused slightly above our heads. Boz deferred to me.

"Window," I said.

Dolly led us through the ballroom. The taffeta drapery swags, the velvet upholstered chairs, the sculpted carpeting—everything was a violent, historical, Vatican red. A hundred tables were covered with white linen, set with dirty crystal goblets and gold-rimmed plates. She deposited us on the porch at a table overlooking the courtyard. Boz held my chair for me. It was too high and my legs were too long. The apron of the table was scraping my thighs, tearing runs in my stockings. My knees kept bumping the table legs.

Dolly filled our water glasses so full that the water lay above the brim like a lid. She set a bread basket before Boz, then adjusted it in fits and starts back and forth between Boz and me. The butter dish she placed at his elbow, half off the table. I understood perfectly: Dolly was fulfilling her role while expressing her rage in quarter inches.

"Something to drink?"

Boz ordered a bottle of expensive champagne. I hadn't been

expecting that. He reached across the table to hold my hand. "Whatever happens," he said, "you have made me happier than I ever dreamed possible." It sounded so eloquent that I tried to ignore its elliptical foreshadowing. I would tell Boz the terrors of my childhood, things that would make him cherish me more. I started to speak. He withdrew his hand.

Dolly was coming at us, dragging a wine bucket across the carpet to our table. She flipped the bottle in front of Boz, too close for him to read. He pushed it away gently and reviewed the label. "Excellent," he said.

She wrapped the neck of the bottle in the folds of her skirt to uncork it. I couldn't believe she was doing that. All the champagne would end up on her dress. She twisted and twisted, then pointed the bottle away just in time. The cork exploded and immediately hit something in the ballroom. She filled our flutes in coarse gushes. "Enjoy," she said tonelessly, and backed away, engrossed in the chipping of polish from her thumbnail.

We clinked glasses. We drank. I thought of something to say that would make him laugh, but I didn't want to tell him anything personal with her standing right there.

"Do youse want to order?" Dolly asked.

"Give us a minute," Boz said.

She walked away with a hairpin in her teeth. She sat at a table behind me and fiddled with her stray hairs. We sipped. We smiled at each other. We looked at our menus. Boz had had Vinnie open the restaurant just for us.

"Waitress," Boz called. Vinnie's wife, right behind me, didn't like to be called that. She remained seated for a defiant interval. When she finally rose and came over, she stood too close, flicking the ballpoint into action in Boz's ear. He gestured to me to order.

"How's the Carbonara?" I asked.

"Good." Dolly's wife's voice could not have been less enthusiastic.

"I'll have that."

She wrote avidly on the tablet. "And for you, sir?"

"The veal."

"Which veal."

"Piccata."

She assessed him. Then she began to scribble. She wrote a great deal, whole sentences it seemed, filling up the tab as if it were a diary entry. Eventually she left.

I had the first sentence of my story ready. It seemed like a good time to tell it, but Boz excused himself. I drank my champagne. I refilled my glass.

Gradually, I became aware of a loss of privacy—Dolly was standing to my side, a flyswatter held rigidly at her side. Her eyes were narrowed intently on the window, where two large blue-black flies with iridescent green wings clung to the glass. The sun had set. The sky was navy blue. Her wrist flexed; she raised the swatter and smashed it against the glass too late. The flies rose from the pane and zigzagged lazily away in opposite directions.

Boz returned, stroking my cheek on the way back to his chair. His aristocratic hands smelled fragrant from the fancy men's room soap. Dolly placed salads before us. Mine looked toxic. I ate a little. "Is everything okay?" he asked, so sincerely that I looked at him closely to see if he meant the salad or the love affair. I felt upset. I excused myself.

❖

I threaded my way around the tables in the red dining room, went down the red hall and found the ladies' room tucked under the spiral staircase. Inside, it was all gold mirrors and black marble. I was not alone—there was a pair of shiny black pumps in one of the stalls. I washed and dried my hands. The red towel was damp and repellent.

The salads had been removed when I returned to the table. Dolly approached noisily, bearing an aromatic tray on her shoulder. She set before me a bowl of cooling pearl-colored pasta, before Boz a lump beneath thick red sauce. "Pepper, madam?" she asked, raising the underside of the giant wooden pepper mill at me, making a rude gesture of it.

"Yes, please."

After two cranks of the grinder, I raised my hand to indicate *enough*. Dolly cranked on and on, producing a steady rain of fresh, pungent pepper bits. "Finito," Boz said firmly, pushing the base of the grinder away so the last few flakes of pepper fell onto the carpet. Dolly receded robotically.

I wound the pasta around the fork. I slipped it into my mouth. I swallowed. I ate delicately, I ate it all. Boz poked at the lump on his plate, then left it there. He looked out the window at the night.

A faint, shrill whine started up somewhere—I couldn't tell where. It could have been a generator high up on the mountain. It could have been a hysteric up in the attic.

A great stretch of time passed without service.

Vinnie appeared in place of his wife. He clasped his hands anxiously together, visibly upset by the sight of Boz's cold, complete entrée. "Is something wrong?" he asked.

"No. Everything was excellent."

"Are you sure," he said, "because at Vinnie's Villa, if there's

sured me, he was not. It seemed a game with him to swallow as much smoke as possible. The butt he flicked away in a neat, wide arc that ended just outside his lot.

Plain Glen left a wife and five children behind in the green house, but people in Dustin felt sorry instead for his mother. "Poor Thea, it's breaking her heart," they said in the post office. Until the doors of the Dustin Presbyterian Church closed for good, the congregation counted on Plain Glen's mother to decorate the nave, which she did using construction paper, glitter, and very little else. Plain Glen's father was a highly respected major landowner, like all the Ritchies before him. Plain Glen's two brothers had no trouble finding reasonable lives and wives, though both had moved to Oklahoma and never came back. Plain Glen's arson could only have its source, people implied (though Viola begged to differ), in his wife, a tiny, squinty-eyed fireball of a woman, a divorcée from West Virginia.

Glorine made it her full-time job to look for a job for Plain Glen. With him in jail, she had nothing to do but get the mail. She drew out her expedition to the post office so long, dropping in at Viola's luncheonette and my gallery for so long, it seemed the children back in the green house were raising themselves. I loved the rich, raunchy twang in her voice and she loved to talk. She told me things that were none of my business, though she was right in thinking, if she did think it through, that she could trust me.

"I tell you," she sang one day. "Sex with him was a one-way street. I felt just like a garbage disposal. I told him so, so I'm not telling you something he don't know. And do you know what he done when I told him? Instead of trying to correct the situation, he disappears to Atlantic City with a woman I know and tells his ma he's looking for work."

The day Glorine got the papers finalizing Plain Glen's sentence, an indeterminate term of three to five years, she came over to the gallery to ask me what *indeterminate* meant. When she understood there was some leeway, she mobilized herself to take on the authorities. The warden had eaten the cake she had baked from scratch without a recipe and patiently towed to Ossining on visiting day. The warden claimed it was their policy. Glorine intended to get back at him by seeing just how early she could get Plain Glen out. Based on the way he had stood in the yard with his back to the house, I wondered if he wanted to get out at all. He was building coffee tables in prison (Glorine was outraged that she couldn't have one); he had three square meals a day; for sex he had "Mary Palmer and her five daughters"—Glorine's Appalachian euphemism for masturbation. I thought it sounded like a good life for Plain Glen. I thought so even before I accepted Glorine's invitation to come visit her.

Plain Glen's year-old twin boys lay in separate, urine-soaked playpens watching game shows. Glorine poured store-brand cola into a yellow Melmac coffee cup for me. Her daughters by her first husband avoided us; they passed through the kitchen once, hugging the wall as if to escape a sudden blow. Her four-year old, Glen Junior, did the opposite. He openly defied Glorine within striking range and remained there at her feet to take his blows. He was wailing from one such whack when Glorine's mother-in-law let herself in through the back door. Her bra straps hung in irritating loops below the caps of her sleeves, grazing the soft flab above both elbows. She placed a jar of homemade tomato jam on Glorine's counter and swept up Glen Junior, cooing, "Uh-oh, did mean old Mommy hurt Grandma's little Princey-Wincey again?" She actually said that.

In response, Glen Junior gritted his teeth and pinched Thea's large, soft upper arms so hard that his cheeks shuddered. She pried away his fingers and he started to kick. She held his knees still while continuing to kiss and coo. I believe she thought she was doing the Christian thing, turning the other cheek. She was there only a few minutes, but before she left she addressed Glen Junior exclusively on a narrow range of topics—the smelly air in the kitchen, the possible brain damage of his half sisters, the high price of cigarettes.

Glorine blew Pall Mall smoke out the door after her and dropped the jam in the garbage. She grabbed Glen Junior by the collar and yanked him into her lap.

"See how she favors him?" she said. "She don't even sneeze at the twins. She thinks they ain't Plain Glen's. That's why she makes me get by on welfare. She don't help at all. She don't know nothing! It's *him* ain't Plain Glen's." Glen Junior beamed at me conspiratorially. "I was three months gone when we met!"

A few nights later I was in the darkroom when I heard a thud. It made the glass in my bathroom window shake. There was an alley a foot wide between my gallery and the house next door. The thudding seemed to be coming from there. It went on for four, maybe five minutes. Elise Tucker had told Glorine her husband lost his temper "on her." I called Glorine to ask what to do. She told me to come watch her kids—she'd take care of it. "I ain't half Irish and half Injun for nothin'," she said.

I walked across the highway to the green house. "They've et," Glorine said when I arrived. "Don't let them tell you they ain't." She walked out the door into the night with her carving knife.

I surveyed the little cluster of humanity before me. Aura and Mae pressed themselves against the kitchen wall until they were as flat as stickers. "Hey, girls," I said. On the kitchen table in their infant seats were the twins. I seated myself uncertainly next to them. Slowly, stealthily backing away from me step by step was precociously masculine Glen Junior. "Hey there, Glen," I said. His facial expression betrayed some mature, fully conceived notion that he was prepared to execute. He backed into the corner of the living room and gathered his hands into fists, dancing in place like a boxer ready to burst out of the corner of the ring. Aura and Mae watched with dull eyes, their mouths hanging open.

"Ding," Glen Junior said. He charged me at breakneck speed, hurling himself fists, feet, knees, and elbows into my lap so that we both fell over backward in the chair.

It was midnight before Glorine returned. The twins were still in their infant seats, wide-awake and on their fourth bottle of lime Kool-Aid. Glorine didn't have milk. Glen Junior was sitting on my foot, hobbyhorse-style, his arms wrapped tightly around my calf. My toes, insteps, shins, and knees were bruised and sore where he'd been jumping, slamming, kicking. My ears were ringing; my head was spinning. His attacks had been frontal; the girls had been devious, darting forth from the wall to yank a strand of my hair, which they admired, or to pinch my arms, then darting back. I felt broken and confused. I may have been in shock.

"You couldn't get them to bed," Glorine observed. Her voice was tired. Her features looked welded firmly, soberly in a mask of defiance and endurance.

"No," I said.

"You're too easy with them." Glorine raised her fist to Glen Junior as if to smash him between the eyes. "Get upstairs before I beat the living shit out of you," she said. He charged past her, escaping the swipe as her hand whirled through the air. Aura and

Mae had already slipped off the counter and were slithering away out of their mother's arm-swinging range. She yanked the bottles out of the mouths of the twins in mid-suck and carried them up the stairs, their heads bobbing awkwardly to one side like broken puppets.

When Glorine came back downstairs, she got out the whiskey. What a beautiful color that whiskey was. I drank two. Glorine's combat expression eventually loosened. "He done a job on her tonight," Glorine said. "I tried to get her to leave and come here. And that's when he got a gun. I left and he followed me. I hid down by the swamp for three hours while he looked for me. He thought I was in your place. He pounded on your front door till I thought it would bust. He smashed in the window in your back door. Don't go in there barefoot, Tammy-girl."

She chugged her shot. In one of her rare lapses, she looked at me with hard-bitten reality and said, "All we done tonight was make it worse for Elise. See what happens when you try to help?"

I did see. I limped back across the highway. I cut my fingers sweeping up the glass. I couldn't sleep.

After that, when I heard thudding I stayed in the darkroom.

All fall, Glorine worked on the warden, doing everything she could think of to get Plain Glen home for Christmas. She waited for the ruling on pins and needles, but policy was policy. Plain Glen had served only three months; he didn't qualify for parole. "Not that he ever helped with Christmas," she said. "He didn't lift a finger. He couldn't wait to get it over with, never even got me a present. His mom give him some Avon products and he put them under the tree."

At least Glorine's efforts had won her a friend. The warden looked forward to her visits. All that winter when Glorine drove up to Ossining on visiting day, she spent more time talking to the warden than she did to Plain Glen.

After twelve months of good behavior, he got a home visit. Glorine cleaned house for the first time in a year. She bought frilly new bedroom curtains. Glorine talked about his homecoming as if everything would be better now: sex, conversation, the kids. I worried for her. Prison did not make most men more domestic. Or more heterosexual.

Glorine cooked Plain Glen his favorite meal, roast beef and mashed potatoes. He spent a few minutes inside. Then there he was again, standing on the property line with his back to the house, flicking his cigarette butt away in that wide, important arc.

It was fall, at dusk, the next time the fire whistle went off. The ugly blast ripped through the hamlet. It almost sounded nostalgic—we hadn't had a good fire around there since Plain Glen was sent away. I was getting gas at Hale's Sunoco. The Dustin Hook & Ladder engine rolled out of the garage. There was room for one more, so I grabbed the handrail and stepped on the running board. The engine swung east on County Route 1, the usual motley fleet of volunteers in its wake.

Roiling clouds of black smoke could be seen clearly over the next hill. The fire was right there, but the roads weren't. We lost valuable time—the route to the property took the fire brigade way north and east before it zigzagged back.

The driver killed the siren as he turned into the driveway. The men uncoiled the hose and ran with it down to the swamp. They had a pump—they hoped there was enough water. The Fedder family was standing there, watching in passive disbelief as their dairy barn was destroyed.

The blaze seduced one wall at a time, licking its way along the beams and floorboards, consuming wood, machinery, and straw with equal interest and appetite. The water came through, but too little too late. The firemen had to content themselves with hosing down the side of the silo so it wouldn't catch. Fire poured up through the timbers, crashing against the sky, loud as Niagara Falls. For one magnificent moment, the structure was transparent. It shuddered briefly, then toppled. The flames multiplied like rats, feeding, gorging on what remained.

There were low voices, prayerful tones, as friends and neighbors offered tools, equipment, and free labor to the family if they wanted to rebuild. One of the firemen was flirting with one of the wives, embarrassing her—she was dying to flirt back. There was rapture in the event.

I had missed Mother's setting our house on fire. I always assumed she had done it in rage. Now I wondered if this great purifying cataclysm wasn't more what she had in mind.

I wanted to write Plain Glen an anonymous postcard saying I understood.

Henry

The facade of Henry's Odds 'N Ends Antiques store was a complex burnished copper color achieved by accident and best seen from a distance. Layers of cheap primary-red asphalt sheathing had been torn away by Henry here and there to see what materials lay underneath—plain brown brick in some places, rust-spotted concrete block in others. He had no sign—an old maple spinning wheel rolled out onto the shoulder of the highway indicated he was open—and no serious electricity, just one bare bulb. No one knew where Henry lived. He seemed to appear in Dustin on his off days or on his way somewhere else, rattling down the hill from the west in his big green van (the engine died at the stop sign every time), opening the shop for an hour or two, then closing again.

I was cutting mats for photographs on a makeshift table—plywood and sawhorses—in back of our stores the first time I saw Henry. "Well, lookie here," he said. He seemed pleased to have a girl for a neighbor. On the narrow white stove, which I had spent the morning scouring, was a pot of freshly percolated coffee. He shoved his hands deep into his pockets and bowed at the shoulders. "Henry Storey," he said.

"Tamara Johanssen." I put down my X-Acto knife and wiped my palms on my jeans, but since he didn't extend his hand, I kept from extending mine.

"Think I smell coffee," he said. He grinned, wrinkling up his nose. His eyes were a bright, impractical blue; one tooth was brown. His long, dirty hair was held off his face by his crushed fedora, worn on the back of his head. You had to look hard to see that he was both young and handsome. I poured him a mug of coffee, which he drank while watching me finish the mat.

"Is that the actual photograph you want to frame?" he asked, innocently suggesting that it might not be such a good idea.

"It's weeds in snow," I said. It was my photograph, taken in art school. "It's *supposed* to be abstract."

"Well"—he laughed—"it *is* that. That's what it is, all right. Hey—know what?" He bent at the waist to study the painted white knob on my back door.

"What?"

"Would you happen to have a screwdriver?"

I handed him the new yellow-handled one I'd bought at the Dustin Agway. The way he held his hands was awkward; I studied him as he applied his strength to the knob mount, expecting him to fail, but he had the screws out quickly. He twisted, then pulled—my whole doorknob, both sides, including the lock, was in his hand. "Would you happen to have a sharp knife?" I stepped inside and retrieved a paring knife. Henry scraped the blade along the painted knob, a few careful strokes, as if he were whittling. "Lookie here! It's glass underneath all that white paint. It's worth money!" He held the mechanism before me proudly. "Do you happen to have any paint remover?"

"No."

"Well, when you get some, you pop over and I'll show you how to strip it, and before you know it, you'll have a beautiful doorknob here."

"Great," I said. He laid the mechanism on the floor just inside the door and wandered over to his store.

The next evening I was sitting on my back stoop, husking corn. Dennis Hale, who fixed cars at his father's Sunoco station by day, was building my darkroom after hours. He had gone earlier for the day, leaving the sweet scent of sawdust in the studio. I'd been to the roadside vegetable stand and come back with half a bushel of tomatoes and a big bag of onions. They were now cooking together slowly in a big pot on the stove. I had just taken my first sip of beer when Henry appeared.

"Evening," he said.

"Evening." I finished the last ear and lit a cigarette.

"Hey, know what?"

"What?"

"You need some chairs back here."

I thought about that for a minute. I wasn't sure what kind of relationship Henry wanted us to have. "That's exactly what my boyfriend says," I said, though the word seemed to frivolize Boz.

Henry seemed relieved. "He's right," he said. "And I got tons of chairs upstairs. I'll give you a good price on a pair. Or you can trade me. I need to get some pictures framed. Would you like to trade?"

I smiled. Barter was my new religion. "Yes."

"Good. Would you like to look at chairs?" I would. I followed

Henry into the back of his store. Big sidesteps were necessary to navigate between the dark shoulder-high stacks of boxes and bins. Everything looked interesting—old tools, fine lace collars, turquoise insulators. "Lookie here—copper!" Henry grinned, lifting up a carriage lamp to show me the reddish gleam where he'd scraped the black paint away. "Worth money! Careful here." The stairway was unlit and doubled as a storage area—the category of wares appeared to be industrial refuse, old lead type, typewriter spools, and a box of terry-cloth bathrobe pockets. "You can have those," Henry said, indicating the pockets, "if you think you can do something with them."

"Thanks," I said, and put one in my pocket.

The upstairs room was stocked to the rafters with furniture of all ages and kinds. Dressers upon dressers, back-to-back sideboards, secretaries, love seats, rockers, tables, and chairs, chairs, chairs. "Maybe you want a stool," Henry said, spinning a three-legged claw-footed piano stool a half-turn. It squeaked mightily. "Or maybe you want a rocker." He plopped himself down in a massive one, suitable for a colonel, but the seat gave out. "Ooops," he said. "That one needs fixing."

"What about these?" I asked Henry, moving toward a stack of lovely, simply proportioned black-lacquered kitchen chairs with high carved backs. They looked like the chairs in my childhood copy of *Goldilocks*.

"You don't want those," Henry said. "Those are German. There's three of them and a table."

"For inside, not out," I said.

"Nope, you don't want them. They've got to go to a dealer." Thinking it was the black I liked, Henry quickly found a black pair and talked me into them. "They're comfortable and you won't care if they get a little rain on them." I helped him haul them down the stairway, one at a time. We set them up in my gravel—one wobbled and the other was cracked. "Tell you what," Henry said. "Would you have any Elmer's glue?" I brought him some. He disassembled both chairs in that awkward but effective manner of his that continued to fascinate me. "Know what?" he said, kneeling in a sea of leg pieces, studying the unpainted tips. "They might be cherry. Have you got any light you can turn on?" The sun was setting. I flicked on the bulb over the back door. He showed me the solid, figured auburn wood. "You're getting the best of this deal." He winked. "Your boyfriend's going to be proud of you. Say, what's that I smell? It smells just like I-talian food."

I invited him to stay for dinner and went inside to boil water. He scraped away at parts of the legs, seats, and backs. "Cherry throughout," he called. It pleased me, bringing out a platter of corn—three apiece—and a big bowl of steaming salted and oiled spaghetti, ladled over with fresh tomato sauce. We ate in silence, me sitting on the stoop, finishing my warm beer, Henry squatting Indian-style in the gravel. The mosquitoes rose in swarms in the glare of the back-door light. Down below in the swamp there was an occasional fat sawing sound from a lone bullfrog. "Never had any spaghetti better than that," Henry said. He had little flecks of tomato sauce all over his cheeks, but when he reached for a paper napkin, it was to wipe the cherrywood dust off his paint scraper before slipping it into his pocket. A chill rose in my blood for an instant—Henry was missing a finger. The way he wore his class ring and held his hand, it was almost impossible to tell.

After he left, I contemplated my two partially scraped chairs sitting legless on their seats. Then I pulled my door shut by the hole where the knob had once been and turned out the light.

I was standing right there by the spinning wheel one Sunday a few months later when the New York City couple paid seventy-five dollars each for all six of the prints I had framed for Henry. They were large old floral lithographs, gauche in their time, but now, between the fading of the ink and the darkening of the paper, quite appealing. I had chosen flat oak frames and delivered them to Henry within a week of our bargain. The couple tried to get the price down, but none of their New York City tricks worked; Henry did not care whether he sold the prints or anything else, ever.

He pocketed the cash in a quick, hoarding gesture. I was annoyed—I almost felt as if a part of it were mine. All twenty-odd pieces of *chair* were still in the driveway. They'd been rained on twice and I'd stacked them under the eaves, hoping nothing would warp. Yet Henry was counting on me for coffee almost every time he rattled down the hill, died at the stop sign, and rolled out the spinning wheel. Likewise, he was dropping by at suppertime at least once a week, promising he'd get to the chairs but never quite doing it. Instead, he would take apart one of my lamps, start refinishing a piece of furniture, remove a porcelain sink handle—then go home, full.

I told myself that I kept feeding him because of his cat food story. He had explained once that after his mother died, he and his father were so poor that they opened a can of cat food in the dark, cooked it, and ate it, thinking it was hash. "Know what?" he had said. "It was pretty good!"

The truth was, I liked having someone to have dinner with. Henry knew my situation—all that summer he was the only one who did. But still, sometimes when I was standing at the stove or doing dishes, I would catch him looking at my legs. His blue eyes looked lonely and practical then. I don't think he was aware of the frequency with which he broke the silence by saying, "People ask what I do for a living—I say I'm a bachelor because it's a full-time job."

When I came back from L.A. after Christmas, Henry was gone. He took off every January to attend a spiritualist camp in the Adirondacks. I missed him.

I complained to Boz. When could we next have dinner together, I wanted to know. He suggested that we go to a bed-and-breakfast upstate. He'd get away somehow. He told me to pick a weeknight after my next period. It hit me like a bucket of cold water—when was my last one? In the holiday confusion, I'd missed one, maybe two. I told him this. He put down the phone and closed the door to his office. "Jesus Christ, I don't believe it," he kept saying. "Are you sure?" And then he told me that his wife was five months pregnant.

A week went by with our talking on the phone every day. Suddenly we did what he called *making a decision.* He made the appointment. I went alone. And I came back even more alone. His life was in order now. Mine was not. I didn't want to see his face after that, although he went to a lot of trouble to make his face available for viewing.

I tried to be mature by cooking nourishing meals for myself, but everywhere I looked, thanks to Henry, I saw something in pieces—my lamps, my doorknobs, my sink handle, and out in back, capped with graying snow, my chair legs—and I lost my appetite. I thought about how I had really wanted those three black Goldilocks chairs with the matching table, and how Henry had selfishly steered me away from them. I asked myself if I had ever gotten what I wanted from a man—or had I always settled for what he had left over?

Henry showed up, clean-shaven and renewed from his retreat. I invited him in for coffee before I realized he had brought a friend, a small, gray-faced man in his fifties with a harsh, persistent cough. I put out cookies and then, because they were so hungry, bread and butter and, finally, more bread, a cold sliced meatloaf, and a jar of mustard. Henry prompted the man to entertain me with spiritualist tales. I was told about the Moving Table, the Perpetually Blooming Rose, and the Dog That Drove. The Dog That Drove sounded suspiciously familiar, like a Ripley's Believe It or Not.

The conversation wore on until suppertime. I was very tired, but when no move was made on their part to leave, I heated up soup and baked a tray of biscuits. They left me out of the conversation as they ate, gently disagreeing as they ranked the invisible guides of the various instructors at the camp. They were hard to understand—their mouths were full of food—but apparently the guides were equipped with varying levels of faculties, sort of like car accessories: the ability to protect from accidents in automobiles but not in airplanes, the ability to contact friends in past lives but only back to the 1300s, and so on.

I had wiped clean the baking sheet and put away the soup pot when Henry pointed out to me that his friend had fallen asleep at the table. Henry suggested that since he had no heat or electricity, the man might spend one night—and I distinctly remember his saying *one*—with me. I laid a sleeping bag on the floor and donated my pillow. Together we eased the man inside the bag. Henry said good night.

I was almost asleep myself when the man coughed himself awake. He asked me for an oatmeal poultice, which I didn't have and had never heard of. He complained that he had woken up because he was sleeping north-south instead of east-west. I picked up the end of his sleeping bag and dragged it a quarter turn, but he still wasn't happy. He wanted something made of iron beneath his pillow—my pillow. I looked through my tools and utensils and offered him a choice of a hammer or a knife sharpener. He took the sharpener, which wasn't iron, and we both went back to sleep.

I expected to hear Henry's van rattle down the hill and die at the stop sign first thing in the morning. He didn't show up by ten; he didn't show up by noon. At four o'clock the man turned on the gas range without lighting it to boil water for tea and almost blew us up. I decided to load him into my car and deliver him to the Wickley Hospital emergency room for treatment of his cough or anything else they could find to treat. Mysteriously, on the way to the hospital, the man stopped coughing and proclaimed himself healed. He asked to be put on a bus to Albany.

The word *moratorium* formed in my mind as I counted out thirty-four dollars for his one-way ticket. There was to be a moratorium on giving men what they wanted, no matter how rude or cruel I felt in the process. It didn't work on Boz. I tried to end it, but I couldn't. I had to see him and he had to see me. A dark shadow had fallen between us, of course. For a while our sex was hurried and superficial. I tried not to need his love, but I did need it and he needed mine.

The moratorium worked a little better with Henry. A week had gone by. I was taking down the local landscape show when Henry appeared at the gallery window, his hands shoved deep into his coat pockets, his shoulders shaking to show me how cold he was. I opened the door a few inches. "Could that be coffee I smell?" he asked.

"Yes, it's coffee," I said. "Just like they have in coffee shops." I shut the door again and went back to work in plain sight of him. He stood outside, shivering and watching me for a quarter of an hour, then he went away. He reappeared the next afternoon with something in his hand. I opened the door a crack. "What's that?" I asked.

"For you," he said, "worth money." On display in the steady palm of his three-fingered hand was an "I Like Ike" button, a handsome sample from the box. I picked up the button. Underneath was the stub of the missing finger. I held his wrist still so I could look at it.

"Could I take one quick picture of this?" I asked.

"You don't want to do that," he said. "My old messed-up mitt. You don't want an ugly old picture like that."

"Yes, I do, Henry," I said. "I do want that."

"Know what?" Henry's eyes were darting around the gallery, trying and failing to find an object to disassemble. "Okay," he said at last. He left his coat on, but he pulled the sleeves up above the wrists and held his hands under the lights. Instead of taking one quick picture, I shot three rolls of black-and-white film. The hair on the back of my neck was tingling. I knew how to make a pair of hands say something. I wanted to do more Dustin hands. I wanted to do Viola's next.

After that, Henry brought me gifts, small ones for coffee, bigger ones for supper. I thanked him, of course, but I'd stopped caring now that I had the shot. The print I ultimately chose from those rolls is still my favorite, even when I see it hung with all the others in the Dustin Hands Series. It's a close-up with the palms down. The angle and the light are just right—the viewers see nothing especially noteworthy about the hands at first, though something fascinates them, compels them to keep looking. When they discover the missing finger, they make a noise—a snort, a little intake of breath, something. They want to show the print to someone else to watch the reaction. Some murmur the title, which pleases me. Each print is titled according to the subject's occupation, and Henry's I call *Bachelor*.

Fran

Franny Mrzoz was a short, stout fist of a woman. As the widow of a failed onion farmer, she was expected to live out her days as a dependent of her successful sister, the nun. Instead, she bought the graceful one-hundred-year-old Dustin Hotel for the back taxes, then squeezed, banged, chopped, and gouged it into an ugly multi-family income property. On this eyesore, she lavished perfect seasonal upkeep.

I was in the luncheonette, sipping coffee with Viola and Glorine one humid July morning when Fran single-handedly toted a two-story wooden ladder out of her storage barn, slammed it up against the side of the house, and climbed the rungs, herky-jerky, like a folk puppet, with a hammer in one hand and a certain look on her face—a look of self-satisfaction and sublimated violence, as if she was so smart that she could hardly stand it. She wore a housedress. She climbed up to the peak of the roof with the claw end of her hammer ready and set about ripping off shingles.

"You've got to hand it to Fran," I said as we watched her out of the window. "She works like a dog."

Viola looked at me as if I'd spoken in praise of child molesting. She shuddered, sending a tremble all up and down her chest and chin.

"A dog at least is a human being," she said. "That woman is a piece of work. As only a Pole can be—and I can say that because I'm Polish. Tell her, Glorine."

Glorine told. Until Fran bought the hotel, the children and dogs of Dustin crossed the grass to get to one another safely. Fran's new fence forced pedestrian traffic onto the highway. Oil trucks and 18-wheelers routinely tore through Dustin on Highway 6 doing sixty-five miles an hour. Within a week two dogs and a cat were dead. The children of Dustin stopped playing with one another whenever they felt like it. They stayed home, waiting until a parent was free to drive them two houses away.

Except for one child. Glorine's fearless four-year old, Glen Junior, continued to cross Fran's property. Fran was ready. She kept a rock in her pocket. She was fast and she was a good shot. She threw it at Glen Junior. She drew blood. Glen Junior picked the rock up and threw it back at *her*. *He* drew blood. He was fast and a good shot, too.

"Okay, okay," I said.

The heat held all that week as we watched Fran replacing faulty shingles. She now had the only good roof in town. I thought she should get points for that, but I kept my mouth shut. Next Fran got out the paint scraper. She scraped and primed. She painted the hotel white. I thought she'd take a break, but after she cleaned the white paint out of her brush, out came the green enamel. Up the ladder she went to paint the shutters.

We watched from the luncheonette window. We had a fan going, trying to stay cool. And there was Fran all afternoon and all the next day, working straight through without a break. A few times I held my breath. Stroking the brush along hard-to-reach louvers, her stocky arm stretched farther than seemed possible, her torso following until the whole of her seemed poised squarely over thin air.

"Fall," Viola commanded her from the safety of the luncheonette, but Fran finished up without mishap. Down the ladder she came. Her paint can still had green paint in it.

"Watch," Viola said. "She'll paint the stones. It's a Polish thing." We all smoked and watched as Franny trudged over to her stone-lined marigold bed and painted the stones.

In autumn the *Wickley Citizen* published a warning to householders to please bag leaves and bring them to the dump—and not, absolutely not to burn. Carbon monoxide fumes from burning leaves were toxic and could induce severe headaches, nausea, and memory loss. Fran raked and burnt.

"Fran," I called, walking home from Glorine's house one evening at dusk. "Burning is bad for you." It was the only thing I seemed to know that she didn't. She looked at me with all the consideration you'd give an insect you could kill now or later, then went back to her pyre, rake handle in hand, tines on high, breathing steadily and unflinchingly of the acrid haze rising into her face. She could have been carved of wood. I fell back into admiring her.

I admired everything in those days. Boz and I were seeing each other excessively then. Bliss made Dustin better. The old PO looked whiter and more dignified, the flag waving in front looked redder and more valiant. The black cat cutouts Scotch-taped to living-room windows struck the right balance between civic and pagan. The straw men dressed in overalls and propped up in front yards, with legs splayed and softening pumpkin heads akimbo, looked as if they, too, had spent the afternoon prolonging delirium.

Halloween came. Glorine called me up to borrow tinfoil. She had run out in the process of wrapping Glen Junior in it. He was the Tin Man. I brought over a new roll of Reynolds Wrap and watched her finish the job.

"What do you say to Tammy-girl?" she said.

"Thank you, Tammy-girl," he said. I had never seen him be polite. He held still, his arms extending straight out at the shoulders while she wrapped around and around with the foil. I had never seen him hold still.

Glorine's daughters, Aura and Mae, were done up in her lipstick and rouge, decked out in her dress-up clothes—beads and earrings, ruffled Mexican blouses worn off the shoulder, midriffs exposed, long filmy skirts hitched up at the waist with cummerbunds fashioned from her first husband's neckties. They were smoking candy cigarettes and twirling around the room. They looked like child prostitutes. "We're Gypsies," Aura said. I was afraid for them.

I stopped at Viola's on the way back to the gallery to buy trick-or-treat candy. Viola was bloated and red-eyed. That morning she'd had a rack full of Hersheys, Snickers, Three Musketeers. Now it was gone. All there was left was a bag of Kraft caramels. "They cleaned you out?" I said.

"Holidays are hard on some of us," she said. Her voice was surly. She was on a sugar binge. Her eyes teared up. I paid for the caramels and left before she could tell me again how she and her sister had been molested by an uncle when they were young.

The caramels were old and hard, too old and hard to chew. I tried to melt them to make caramel apples, but they were too old and hard to melt properly. I dipped the apples the best I could and set them out on a tray.

At dusk I lit my pumpkin and sat in the display window of my gallery, waiting for Dustin's little ghosts and goblins to come floating through the night up to my door for loot. No one came. I called Glo. "Where is everybody?"

"Oh, they're all home." It was the vigilante voice, low and calm, confident of revenge. "It seems that Mrs. Mrzoz is anticipating a little local vandalism."

Fran was protecting her new paint job. Last Halloween, unknown persons had egged the hotel.

"She's a-sitting on the crossroads with a shotgun," Glorine said. "A shotgun."

"She's aimed it at Lucy Tucker. Lucy Tucker is six. She cocked it at me. My kids wait all year for this. Don't nobody take away *my* kids' Halloween without paying for it."

Erotic fulfillment had lent me a false sense of immortality. I walked out to the crossroads with a flashlight. Fran was sitting in a lawn chair in an Admiral Byrd parka with the shotgun lengthwise on her lap. "Fran," I called. "It's Tamara." I turned the light on my face to identify myself.

She raised the rifle, settled the butt into her shoulder, and sighted down the barrel at me. I took a step forward. She fired. The shot sprayed over my head, tearing into the stop sign with a zing, lodging in the telephone pole down on County Route 1. The sound of the explosion kept echoing, bouncing around in the distance from field to field. I stumbled back a step, my ears ringing, my body in shock. All the way to my front door, I kept backing up,

tripping over my own feet in a mincing, cowardly, graceless display, my veins shrill with survival. I was converted.

Two of the caramel apples I ate for dinner. Then I ate two more for dessert. In the morning the remaining apples were naked and red, sitting in a pool of lumpy cold caramel. I fell apart.

"Someone has got to do something," I said to Viola. We both looked at Glorine. She was sucking on her Pall Mall as if it were a multiple vitamin in smoke form. She seemed a little quiet.

On election day, when Fran was in the Presbyterian church voting for the Republicans, someone slashed the rear tires of her prized heavy-duty Chevy truck. She came out into the parking lot and saw her four-ton vehicle sitting on its axles. The noise she made was like no noise I'd heard before or have heard since. It was high-pitched and unnatural, a shrill multilayered scream, like brakes on a runaway semi heading downhill.

Behind Fran's barn was an Airstream trailer surrounded by a mound of junk for sale. I had walked past this blight for months and had only recently learned that a man lived in there. He was Dustin's dog warden, and his name was Marshall Jim.

Marshall Jim's trailer was illegal—there was no certificate of occupancy—but the land beneath it was his. The half acre, left to him by his mother, included the hotel driveway and storage barn. To compensate him for his right-of-way, Fran fed Marshall Jim and his dog, Wallace.

Wallace was a sweet old swaybacked coonhound who liked to spend his days lying half in, half out of a large elaborate doghouse. Wallace's beautiful eyes were aglow with a lifetime of love and affection for Marshall Jim. Marshall Jim had gone all out for him, siding the doghouse with real aluminum siding, installing real glass windows, and "shingling" the roof with colorful carpet sam-

ples. NOT 4 SALE was painted on the side of the doghouse in white
paint to distinguish it from the items for sale around the trailer: a
dozen tires (each marked $4), a rowboat (probably the best buy at
$100), an adding machine ($8.50—marked down from $9).

Fran banged on the trailer door, shrieking for Marshall Jim to
come out.

We watched from the luncheonette window. "Will he?" I
asked. I was hyperventilating.

"Probably not," Viola said. "When did he last come out,
Glorine?"

"Eight years ago," Glorine said. "We had a tornado and he lost
his television signal. He'd been waiting five years to watch Eddy
tell Kevin that Robert was not his real father. So Jim comes over to
my house."

"Will she stop banging on his door?" I asked. I needed a seda-
tive.

"Only when Marshall Jim arrests someone," Viola said.

Glorine inhaled long and hard. She exhaled that way, too. She
was taking a bow. I felt better. I had a friend who could take on a
killer.

Fran was scary. Her endurance was synthetic—it had no
wrinkle or inconsistency, powered as it was by a single incorrect
belief: that Marshall Jim was a law-enforcement official. Fran took
a break for lunch, then went at it again, pounding and shrieking.
By dusk, Wallace was cringing in the rear of the doghouse. "Stop
the racket, Fran," Detering yelled at her from the road. "You're
upsetting the dog." A number of us gathered with Detering to
back him up in case she went for the shotgun. The wives spoke to
me briefly to make up for my being shot at by Fran.

In the morning Wallace was dead. He lay in the dirt in front of the doghouse, eyes half closed, lips distorted and hard and blue. Half his food was still in his bowl. We gathered around the doghouse. Someone had to inform Marshall Jim. Detering knocked on the trailer door. "Say, Jim," he called through the aluminum. "The dog looks poorly."

Marshall Jim came forth. He wore a white tank T-shirt. His gun belt was hitched up high on his waist. His hair rose off his forehead in an abrupt greasy pompadour. His facial features seemed compressed into one central feature, like the behind of a sheep. Instead of a jacket, he wore a blanket thrown over his shoulders like a stole.

We watched with morbid embarrassment as he knelt down in the dirt and petted Wallace's cold head. "Come on, buddy," he said. He lifted a little gook out of the corner of Wallace's eye and flicked it into the dirt. "Come on, buddy," he said again.

Next door, Franny Mrzoz trudged out to her trash can with a neatly tied bundle of garbage. She whipped off the metal lid, deposited it, and whisked her hands clean. "Francine Mrzoz," Detering said. "You didn't stoop to this, I hope."

Franny got that look on her face as if she were so smart that she could hardly stand it. "Maybe I did and maybe I didn't," she said.

The men of Dustin went home to get their shovels. They dug a grave behind the trailer. They buried Wallace. The raw mound of fresh earth was painful to view. Glorine brought over plastic flowers to decorate the grave. Before we could stop her, she called out to Marshall Jim to come see it. We were all glad he stayed inside. We held a little service. Detering said a few words about Wallace of the "too good for this earth" variety. We all murmured, "Amen." Viola invited everyone back to the luncheonette for coffee. A dog with a heart of gold had made us all more human.

The next day Fran got new tires. She wrapped her shrubs with burlap. She put up snow fence along her driveway, really Marshall Jim's driveway. I thought her chores were done for the winter, but something under the eaves got her attention. There she was, charging out of the barn with the heavy wooden ladder, slamming it up against the side of the building, climbing up the rungs, all with a cone of tar paper and a match. A great tumorous cakey hornet's nest had formed high in the eaves. At the top of the ladder, she lit the wide end of the tar-paper cone and waved it under the nest.

Half a dozen drowsy hornets glided out. Fran flicked the thing to the ground with a single jab of her screwdriver. Down she climbed with nary a sting. *Fall,* I thought as I watched her this time.

In March, Glorine was called home to West Virginia for a family funeral. She hired two teenage black sisters from Hapsburg to babysit for her five kids. Their first morning in town, they bundled up the kids and took them outside to play.

Fran was ready. She hit the younger girl in the shin with a rock. The older girl got it in the forehead. Glen Junior broke free, climbed Franny's fence, ran up, and bit her hard in the leg. Oddly, Fran just stood there and took it like a man. The girls called their mother to come and take them home.

My neighbor Elise Tucker took the girls. Her husband had left her, so her place was safe. Glorine's mother-in-law took the twins. She tried to take Glen Junior, but he wouldn't go. He stayed alone in the green house, eating peanut butter with his finger right out of the jar and coloring on the walls.

Fran was evil. I could see it. I could say it. I looked forward to what would happen next when Glorine got back. But Glorine was sick with grief. She was too tired and too upset, it seemed, to settle the score with Fran. She had gone back to West Virginia to try to straighten out her family feud.

In April, Fran's bulbs were the first to come up. Then snakes began to multiply and divide at an alarming rate in her cellar. Fran mixed up an old-world remedy consisting of vinegar, baking soda, and ammonia, soaked rags in it for twenty-four hours, then laid the rags about the seams where the cellar walls met the ground. A few snakes reacted by migrating upward to the cool, dark, damp space beneath Fran's kitchen sink. The remainder of the snake population continued to flourish.

Fran hired an exterminator. He was mystified at how so severe a degree of infestation had developed in only two months' time. Even more curious—he'd never seen this type of snake so far north before. He poured tar in the holes in the cellar floor, sealed the chinks in the loose cement between stones, and set snake traps baited with poison.

There were many casualties. But many survived. They kept turning up, surprising Fran where she least expected them. Her maintenance schedule went to pot. She no longer went anywhere with that look on her face. The downstairs tenants moved out in May. The upstairs tenants lasted until June. Fran was the last to go. She could take heat and cold, rain, sleet, and snow, carbon monoxide, hornets, and heights—but not this. She crossed herself and moved in with her sister the nun. The multifamily building on the Dustin crossroads went up for sale. Shirley Girt was at the wheel again.

Detering

Detering ruled the post office with a mixture of fawning and intimidation. Both postures were means to an end: whatever a person thought was private, he wanted to know more about. He had no prejudice as to category; he was like a psychotherapist with bad will. The post office itself co-conspired. It was tiny and dark, a rickety saltbox built of white clapboard on the edge of the highway in the 1890s, when Dustin was a major stop on the Erie-Lackawanna Railroad. Detering's window was right out of a Hollywood Western, narrow and high with strong hickory bars and a "bowl" depression carved into the pine counter to slide pennies in and stamps out. The original post-office boxes were still intact, solid brass with beveled glass doors. The combination dials were also brass and nicely machined. They were beautiful boxes, but they were a century too small. For every magazine, newspaper, catalog, or oversize piece of junk mail, Detering had to sort a yellow CALL AT WINDOW FOR PACKAGE card into the box, an inconvenience for which he made us peons pay in units of gossip—he didn't care how long the line got.

The fawning he reserved for the rich, the landed, the power-ful—there was one of each. They double-parked on the shoulderless highway, ran into the PO with their big cars idling, and cut the line. Detering always had their neat, complete bundle ready and waiting. He called his well-wishing after them in a voice as honeyed and insincere as the wolf in Little Red Riding Hood. When they were gone, he gloated, his status elevated by the contact, as if he, however briefly, were now rich, landed, or powerful, too. Occasionally they took time to linger. Detering weaseled confessions out of them. Then he let us in on what he knew, parsing out juicy tidbits as he saw fit. He traded in all sizes and brands—no shame was too big or too small.

I entered the PO my first afternoon as a Dustin resident reeking of tragedy, flight, and the potential for sex. I could hear him back there on the private side of the post office reading the newspaper. Each big, crisp page of the local edition snapped tight as he turned it. "Hello?" I called. He made me wait.

Above me, next to the portrait of George Washington, was an official black-and-white army photo of the Fighting 121st, a World War II platoon stationed in France. I studied it. When Stanley Detering finally chose to appear behind the bars of the window, I tapped on the photo right on his face. "I see you," I said. He was in the front row, second from left. He looked barely twenty. Today, his hair still rolled in waves away from his forehead. His chin was still flat, his jaw square. He looked the same except the jaunty G.I. glint in the eye had soured, the ambiguous smile had slipped a quarter inch to the side and was now snide.

His eyes slid over my chest. I felt braless and promiscuous. "I see you, too," he said, and slipped an application form into the bowl of the wooden counter. He disappeared.

"Ready," I said. Name, address, phone—it was hardly a form. But Detering was busy again, thumbing through a catalog, calling an 800 number. A quarter of an hour passed as he selected pleated corduroy trousers in two new fall colors from L. L. Bean. This could have waited—it was July. He then allowed the customer service representative to conduct a brief customer satisfaction survey. He rated the experience excellent.

Finally he appeared, relaxing in the barred window with his pipe, avoiding eye contact as he scraped the bowl clean, filling it leisurely with pinches of aromatic cherry tobacco, tamping it down ever so thoroughly, lighting it, puffing. He puffed ten times, then took the pipe out of his mouth. "So," he said. "What brings you to our fair metropolis?"

While I hesitated in answering, he sized me up. He read things in the eyes, the hair, the face, and sniffed a good-size secret, something worth hunting, worth the kill, something he could hang and feed on all winter.

"The feed store?" I was asking him, not telling him.

"You aim to feed or be fed?" he said.

I laughed the terrible laugh of the victim trying to sound relaxed. "Yes," I said, and left it at that.

He picked up my form. He frowned at my name.

"Running away from a man?" he said, as if he were reading it there. He'd been at it forty-six years—this was what brought women between the ages of sixteen and sixty to Dustin to rent.

I hesitated again. I had just read that people who hesitate before they answer a question are about to lie. I kept quiet, but I turned red.

He smiled his *gotcha* smile. Our first round and he had already scored big without even trying. He stamped my form APPROVED and assigned me box no. 1, combination one, two, three. It seemed all these years, he'd been saving Dustin's most babyish address for me.

"What's this, your first checking account?" Detering said one afternoon, holding up the incriminating insufficient-funds envelope from the bank as if showing the jury Exhibit A. I said nothing. After three weeks in Dustin, I had learned that Detering's questions were trick questions and could only be answered in his favor. A check had bounced and it wasn't my fault. I didn't apologize or explain.

Detering barked up the money tree for a while. He couldn't figure out where I was getting the funds to renovate. My sister's snow-white no. 10 envelopes with their important colorful television network logo slipped in monthly below his radar. He sniffed some more, but the money trail grew cold and Detering abandoned it. He moved on to sex.

"You and Henry spend a lot of time together," he said one morning, a reasonable first try. He handed me a large manila envelope without letting go of his end. We both tugged a little.

"He says you make good coffee," he said. Silence from me.

"Does he like it black or with cream and sugar?"

People were standing around, waiting for my reply.

"She gives him coffee every morning, but she doesn't know how he likes it," Detering announced to the other residents in line. Then he let go of his end of the envelope and I lost my balance. I stumbled back a step. People laughed.

I avoided rush hour after that. I tried getting the mail when no one else was there. "What's in Wickley?" Detering asked me one day. I forgot to be silent. "Work," I said. He wouldn't have asked the question if my excited car trips north on Highway 6 past the post office three days a week at 1:30 P.M. had the rhythm of work.

"Really!" he said. "At the corner of WALK and DON'T WALK?"

He stuck to the sex angle all summer. In the fall my afternoon car trips went south. From his perspective, they stopped. He snooped a bit without success. I was mum.

One afternoon I went in to get the mail after Boz and I had been together at the lake cottage. Detering picked up the scent again, detecting the additional happiness in my body as accurately as if he'd been watching us. A cluster of retired old codgers with terrible breath who looked as though they were sewn together at the elbows backed out of my way as I approached the window with my yellow card.

"Well, well, well," Detering said. "Aren't you looking just like the cat that ate the canary." I gave him the card.

"Who's missing a canary," Detering said. "That's the sixty-four-thousand-dollar question."

The codgers laughed their croaky smokers' laughs. He gave me my package.

"Tweet, tweet," Detering called as I walked out the door.

The approval for the new post office came through. Ground was broken on the land behind Marshall Jim's trailer. Excavators cranked up their backhoes and rolled up to the site. Detering abandoned his post frequently, walking up to the site to supervise. He was getting everything the way he wanted it—floor plan, windows, counters, equipment. Approval must have been missing from his career. He was taking this one as broadly and personally as possible.

"Come on up Monday for the pouring," he said to me. He had my oversize mail ready, no waiting, no toying. His voice was round and warm, filled with good cheer, not narrow and sticky with camouflaged traps.

I paused to see if there was a catch.

"Free coffee," he said with a foolish grin. His face looked smarter when he was mean.

The whole town came out. The famous Valducci Brothers of Sussex, New Jersey, were doing the concrete. Viola closed the luncheonette to attend. For the occasion, she'd dieted for two days and placed large Spanish combs in her hair. Dressed spiffily in his new L. L. Bean corduroys, Detering waited on the crossroads to direct the Valduccis to the site.

At ten A.M. sharp, they rolled into town in a new pin-striped cement mixer, two Valduccis in the cab and two more hanging off the running boards. Their curls were ink black, their bodies stout and muscular, their personalities by Dustin standards were outrageously flirtatious. They worked in concert like a circus troupe, conferring with the sign language of their profession. A nod of the chin and the belly of the mixer spun. A winding of the wrist and the mix poured forth. Cool, grainy, gray cement rolled down the jointed trough, filling the air with the primal, encouraging odor of clay. The Valduccis tamped, they patted out air bubbles, they stroked their buttery mix into the forms. In motion and at rest, they oozed grace.

Sucking in her stomach and throwing back her shoulders, Viola restlessly scanned the crowd of onlookers. She was looking for someone in particular. When Dave L. Garson arrived late, I saw Viola's lips quiver. Dave crept up behind Elise Tucker and grabbed her waist, scaring her, though she seemed to be expecting him, wearing an uncharacteristic blue bow in her hair. Viola's face fell.

When the forms were filled and leveled, the Valduccis backed their truck around to pour a parking lot. We followed them. A neat L-shaped form with space for fourteen cars had been constructed with two-by-fours. A twist of the wrist. Down the trough rolled the sweet cement. In unbuckled knee-high black rubber boots, the Valduccis stood in six inches of slowly hardening concrete, raking it flat. Everyone was taken with Bambi, the finisher. He knelt on a neat square of plywood with a serrated trowel in each hand. Working his arms like windshield wipers, he combed the final surface texture into the parking lot. Never in Dustin had anything more prosaic been accomplished with a poetry so European.

Viola missed the whole Bambi routine, watching heartbroken as over and over Dave L. Garson threw Elise Tucker's one-year-old baby high up into the air. Every time the baby was airborne, his laughter rang out, raucous, wild, and free. He was too young to know the rules—you don't laugh at Dave L. Garson. Viola's combs fell out of her hair. Her lipstick smeared. She listed starboard as she dragged herself back to the luncheonette like a giant wilted flower.

"He's a pervert," I informed Viola. "I came this close to calling the police on him."

She turned on me. "When was this?"

"A couple of months ago."

She eyed me up and down, a rival. "He doesn't like skinny girls," she informed me, as if I were mistaken.

Detering was so involved in the construction progress that he seriously neglected his prying. I enjoyed my new leeway and relaxed. Too much, it seems, or else I wanted to get caught as so many criminologists claim we furtive antisocial types do. That was when I wrecked my car on the private road that led to the private lake cottage where Boz and I did our very private things.

I walked in circles, displaced in my own home, trapped and exposed, netted, labeled, and still twitching, while up at the construction site, Detering told the town what he knew. The way he stood, literally turning his back on me, bothered me more than it should have. The little ragged, poor, bent people of Dustin stood with their backs to me, too. For hours, it seemed, though my sense of time was off. Were they repeating everything in an endless loop? There wasn't that much to say.

Viola knocked on my door Sunday morning after church. "I am calling on you to officially disown you," she said. Her red wool coat was fresh from the dry cleaner's. This seemed to lend formality to her speech. "I understand you're a woman of the nineties, but I never *ever* expected this from the likes of you. I really cannot continue our association."

Glorine alone braved the ban on socializing with me. She came to my back door that evening with whiskey and cigarettes. "Welcome to the Slut Club!" she said. I told her the whole story.

"Don't I feel like a fool, bragging to you 'bout sex I had a year ago when you been getting it right here and didn't say nothing."

"He's married," I reminded her.

"The first man what had me was married, too—to my own mother." She told me her whole story. We smoked some more. We drank whiskey. "Does he eat you?" Glorine asked on her way out the back door. Suddenly I felt prudish—my chin flexed backward into my throat. "He does, don't he," she said. "See, that's what I miss. My first husband would do it, but Plain Glen, he won't."

❖

Carless. Shunned. I sat on the back stoop to smoke cigarettes as a way of getting out of the house. Glorine did me the favor of fetching the mail for a week, then she got the flu. I had to face Detering. No matter what he asked, I promised myself I would not answer.

People were there, gossiping. Their voices tapered off when I walked in. I worked my combination in silence. Of course, there was a yellow card in my box. I queued up at the end of the line. Everyone bowed out of my way, and Detering took me next.

"Here you be," he said, handing me a postcard.

"That's it?" I said, breaking my rule.

"What were you expecting—something like so?" He measured fourteen inches in the air with open facing palms. "Because from what I hear, you get a lot of legal-size now."

People laughed. I looked at Detering. He had that cruel *gotcha* look in his eye. From the depths of my being, I wished him ill. I wished with all my heart and soul that only harm, only bad things, would come to him. As I walked out, the local wives laughed after me while their husbands fixed me with hot, appreciative sidelong stares. They each wanted to be next.

Glorine had sworn to keep the details of my love life a secret, but talking to Viola, she let on that sentimental transactions had occurred between me and Boz. There were gifts, ceremonies, pledges. There was love—not the compulsive, dissolute bad behavior alleged by Detering. Viola felt left out. She came to my door in a repeat performance of equal formality, reversing her position.

"I have judged you unfairly," she said. "If you can see your way to forgive me, I will defer to you on the subject of promiscuity wherever it arises, at the local, state, and national level."

I gave her the whole story, and she must have been inspired. She left me in the dust, slutwise, a few months later by running away with a black man. Roman had had his eye on her for years. He managed the migrant workers at the apple orchard. He watched her drink alone at night. He thought she was beautiful. He boldly told her at least once a year that anytime she saw his light on and needed company, to come on down. On December 10 she did.

They ran away to Wickley, staying with Viola's divorced friend, Kitty, in Kitty's apartment over the furniture store. Viola left love-drunk messages on my answering machine. I played them for Glorine.

"When he kissed me, I didn't care what color he was."

And "Once you go black, you never go back."

And "Never have I known such complete happiness, body and soul. You don't know what you're missing. Glorine, either."

"I might throw up," Glorine said, listening. "In West Virginia we don't ever mix with coloreds."

"Say blacks."

"We don't have no blacks down in West Virginia," Glorine said. "All we got is coloreds."

"Glorine!" I said. "Besides, what about you and your father. That's really crossing a line."

"Sometimes it is for the best," she said. She was proud of her past. It made her feel superior. Some shrink might someday have a whee of a time with Glorine, but until that day, Glorine would continue to draw nothing but self-esteem from any attention she'd ever received.

Viola and Roman lasted a month. They ran out of money. They had a tiff. He drove home alone in his Eldorado to his shack. She came back to Dustin at noon on Christmas Eve in a taxicab. The luncheonette was open again. Glorine and I went over for coffee.

"Welcome to the Slut Club," Glorine hooted.

"I am nothing if not a Roman-tic," Viola said with a smoky new confidence and a rich awareness of the pun.

Viola's husband, Bud, was grateful to have her back. But the hamlet gave her the treatment, the carefully orchestrated public humiliations from Detering, the mean cackling from the wives, though the looks from their husbands were not looks of desire but of distaste and racial defeat. "I could care less," Viola said. "I got what *I* wanted for Christmas."

On St. Patrick's Day, Detering moved into the new plant. Architecturally, the completed post office resembled nothing more than a glorified garage. Daylight poured into the facility on all four sides. A simple waist-high counter divided the public side from the private. The boxes were large and aluminum with key-operated locks. People helped themselves to their own mail now, and all of it fit.

The mail was easily sorted by nine. Detering spent the rest of the day trying to hold court in his expensive new Posturepedic swivel chair. But the new post office didn't back him up the way the old one did. People came and quickly went. They talked outside in the parking lot as a group, not inside to Detering one at a time. There was a backlash against Detering. People could see how much he'd meddled. Their secrets were now staying secret. Their confidential envelopes hadn't been opened and sealed shut again. The checks for Franny Mrzoz's welfare tenants were no longer a week late. Detering had stopped withholding the official NYS envelopes just to watch them squirm and to punish Fran.

By April Fools' Day, Detering had back trouble. The pain seemed to start in his legs, but it wasn't sciatica—he'd had that and it was worse. Detering blamed his mattress. He blamed forty-six years in the old PO. He blamed World War II. He wanted to talk about it, but no one wanted to listen except Glorine. She spent half her day with him, baked him cookies, cakes, and pies. She leaned on the counter for hours at a time, filling his ear with the stories of her life, then tiptoed out when he snoozed.

Through the open window most of the afternoon, we could see him puffing rhythmically in his chair, his breath just short of a snore, his legs crossed in the feminine manner at the knee. One sock drooped, revealing a stretch of bluish skin tracked with multiple varicose veins. His head bobbed limply forward, his arms folded across his potbelly.

"Sis doing okay?" Detering would ask respectfully if he had sorted one of Nora's snow-white no. 10s into my box.

"Fine, thanks," I'd say on my way out the door.

One hot summer afternoon Detering detained me to ask my advice on a risky new back operation he'd seen on Nora's network. Cement was injected in weak or soft discs to stabilize them. I discouraged him from going ahead with it. I told him that the long-term research wasn't in yet, that in several cases the cement had dislodged and couldn't be removed. Those patients were in more pain than before.

He stood up to thank me, wincing terribly in the process. He pawed my forearm in gratitude as I walked out the door.

Had wishing him ill worked? If I knew such a thing were possible in six short months' time, I would never have wasted a wish from the depths of my being on something bad for Detering. I would have wished for something lasting for myself.

Glorine

The rap on the windowpane in my back door was weak and un-familiar. I was dressed for Sunday evening yoga class, running late, so it was mildly annoying to look up and see a tiny black cotton dress glove poised against the glass. Glorine was home from her daddy's sickbed in West Virginia. I would have to explain my rush and explain it before she even got one word out. Glorine had a way of telling a life story in one uninterruptible sentence. I threw on my sheepskin coat and grabbed my car keys.

"Glo!" I said, opening the door. "I was just on my way out to yoga class."

A sharp wind zigzagged between us, pressing my coat against me and grabbing the open throat of my white cotton yoga shirt—March was going out like a lion. Glorine was silent. She was wearing a gray dress coat I'd never seen; the black veil over her face snapped eerily at her features in the wind. I felt terrible—obviously there'd been a funeral. "Then give me a smoke before you go, Tammy-girl," Glorine said softly. "I smoked all mine driving home."

"I'm all out, Glo," I said. "I'm cutting back." She looked at me with disbelief. "It's one of the benefits of yoga," I said. "You start to lose the craving." This wasn't entirely true. I had two cigarettes in my purse and I wasn't about to give either one up. They were helping me stay off tranquilizers.

"Jesus, Mary, and Joseph," she said. The grief in her voice was sharp. "Where am I going to find a cigarette? Viola is closed and you quit." I felt ashamed.

"Come in and sit a minute," I said. "I'll make you a quick cup of tea. I'll be late." She was stiff from driving or worry or something; she moved as if she were one piece, sitting at the edge of the chair with her elbows on the table, not removing her coat or veil. I hurried the tea, pouring hot but not boiling water over the tea bag. "Honey or sugar?" I asked, placing the pottery mug between her tiny black-gloved hands.

"You got Jack Daniel's?"

I shook my head no.

"Anything, then." I passed the sugar bowl to her. She measured in three heaping spoonfuls, stirred the mess, and removed the tea bag. She tried to drink, pressing the mug to her lips and getting a mouthful of black veil. "Get this off me!" she cried, spitting it out. I jumped to her side, found two corners of the veil and held them straight out over her face like an awning. "Where do you want it?" I asked.

"Back." I half rolled, half piled the veil back over her hair, which badly needed washing.

"He didn't make it, Glo?"

"They called and said he took a turn for the worse. They said he wanted to see me. That was just a story they made up—he was already in the morgue."

"The morgue, Glo!"

"They went in and took all his things. They had no money to bury him decent. So they called me."

"You." Glorine was living on welfare, supporting five children on food stamps. Plain Glen had another ten months in prison. Still, she was the rich sibling.

"I tell you—I can't believe I come from such scum." Her face was thinner and grayer than I'd ever seen it. She looked like a rat. "He looked awful, when I first seen him. His face was all puffy and white like that mold you get on tomato paste. Worse—he looked scared. I couldn't let no morgue bury my pa. If ever a man needed help getting to the other side, it was him. So."

"So you made the arrangements?"

"I had to borrow a thousand dollars from—" She flicked her head up the road at her mother-in-law's large Colonial home.

"From Thea?" I was impressed. Glorine's greatest luxury, besides conversation, was her flamboyant refusal to be changed or affected by Thea Ritchie's suggestions, criticisms, and insults.

"She wired me the money. But now I got to straighten up and fly right."

"Straighten up and fly right?"

She looked at me dead-on. "No more afternoons at the luncheonette."

"All we did was talk."

"That don't matter. Viola is drinking again. You're on her shit list, too. I can't associate with you."

"Me," I said. A day without Glorine was inconceivable. That voice was my antidepressant. I quoted back her famous claim. "Nobody tells you what to do or who to do it with."

"I gave my word," she said.

"We'll sneak across the highway at night to talk."

"When I pay her back, maybe," she said. "Which I don't know how I'm going to do."

"Jeez," I said. "Thea!" I couldn't believe Glorine would ask her for anything.

"Where else am I going to get a thousand dollars?" Glorine looked at me pointedly. "If *ever* a man needed a Christian burial . . ." she said.

"You did the right thing." I felt hurt. I fussed with my coat to show I was ready to leave.

"You know it and I know it," she said, her voice loaded with qualification.

"Why—what happened?"

"Do you got all night? Because if I was to start at the beginning, it would take all night."

"What's the gist?"

"The what?"

"What's the main thing?"

"The main thing"—Glorine grew stern, tapping her black gloved finger on the table as she spoke, defending her position—"is that the death of a parent is no time to fight. Over every last little thing."

"Who fought?"

"Everything I wanted to do, the five of them would squawk about."

"Maybe they were upset?"

"Five to one, Tammy? On every last little thing? I had to kick all five of them out of the funeral home. I told them they couldn't come back until Pa was ready. So when they come back and they seen the face filled in and fixed up like I wanted it, and when they seen the haircut and the manicure which I wanted, and when they seen the suit which I wanted and when they seen the red satin lining with the buttons which I wanted, do you know what they said?"

I shook my head no.

"Hector, my brother, says, 'You got New York money we don't even know about. Why don't you spend it on the living?' He picks up this crucifix, Hector, which I have put around Pa's neck, and he tells Mr. Hinks to take it off—'We're not Catholic. We're Baptist,' he says. It's true, Pa hated the church. But I wanted him to have something with Jesus on it. The only thing I could buy with Jesus on it was a crucifix. So, Mr. Hinks goes to remove the crucifix and I say, 'Don't touch that, Mr. Hinks.' And he don't. Because *I* am paying. So Hector says to me, 'Glorine, if'n you think we don't know about you and Pa, you're wrong. All these years you thought he done it 'cause he liked you best. He never gave two shits about you. Behind your back, you know what he did? He laughed at you.'"

Glorine drank down the tea and ate the sugary mixture at the bottom. "They don't come to the service," she said. "And they don't come to the cemetery. So it's me and the minister standing there. *A*-lone. He says ashes to ashes and dust to dust and I pick up a piece of dirt, thinking to myself this is the last piece of West Virginia I ever want to touch the rest of my miserable life, and I throw it on the coffin.

"I get in my car and start to drive back and every time I look out the window, this one hill in the distance reminds me of Pa's nose. Only way I could keep my car on the road instead of driving off the cliff was by singing, 'Shall We Gather at the River.' I sang that song all the way home."

A soft white gauzy beauty, pink at the edges, had filled Glorine's features as I watched; I couldn't move.

"You did the right thing," I said. "Everything you did was the right thing to do."

She picked up the tea bag and squeezed it. "Think if I dried this out, I could roll it up and smoke it?" She grinned. I thought she was joking, but she put the tea bag in her coat pocket as she stood up. "I've done it before," she said. "I have smoked all kinds of things, just to have some smoke to suck on. Your sister okay?"

I nodded yes, making the long story as short as it could get.

"You go ahead, Tammy-girl. Don't let me keep you."

"You sure you're okay?"

"Nothing's going to squash me. Who knows? Maybe when I straighten up and fly right, I'll get a job and pay Ma back and go to yogey class with you." I tried to picture Glorine and me side by side in the position they call the Plow, asses in the air, legs stretched straight out over our heads. "Feel the energy pulsing in the chakras," the instructor would say. "Feel the universe in every cell."

Glorine walked to the back door. My fingers were nearly welded to my car keys. When she stepped out into the wind, the veil was snatched off her head and jerked away into the night. "Good night, Glo," I called, watching her silhouette move toward the highway. She waved American Indian–style, raising an L-shaped arm without looking back.

I sat in the dark of the car for a minute. Then, while I still could, I did the right thing. I drove to the 7-Eleven in Hapsburg, the only place for ten miles where you could buy cigarettes on a Sunday night, and bought Glorine a carton of Pall Malls. We would sit down together and chain-smoke for hours.

When she answered the door, I slapped the carton into her arms. "Okay, Glo," I said. "Start at the beginning."

The Doctor

Everyone knew the Doctor was wealthy; everyone knew he was a hunter. Still, as we pored over the huge quarter-page classified ad listing items for sale at his estate auction, it appeared that the Doctor was wealthier and more of a hunter than anyone had imagined. Over the years, the postmaster had delivered packages to the handsome native-stone house. Standing at the open door while the Doctor signed for things, Detering glimpsed guns on the wall, but the complete listing floored even him. *Winchester, Winchester, Winchester*—for the two weeks leading up to the auction, those syllables echoed on the crossroads of Dustin like a macho susurrus.

There were hunting and fishing trophies beyond expectation; beaver pelts; a stuffed red fox; trophy saltwater fish, including a record marlin; numerous mounted stag heads, one with a sixteen-point rack. And there was the bear rug, head and claws intact.

The yellowed newspaper clipping was still taped to the wall in the luncheonette, the Agway, the Sunoco station. DUSTIN MAN BAGS RECORD BEAR read the headline. It was the only three-hundred-pound black bear taken in the Catskill Preserve in years, and it had been taken by the Doctor. The photograph showed him standing next to his cream-colored Mercedes. On the roof, rising like an inert holy mound from the heart of the forest, was the bear. The Doctor was smiling a careful, ambiguous, intelligent smile— not the usual hunter's hundred-watt grin. Of course, the Doctor wasn't really a Dustin man, or he wouldn't have been driving a Mercedes.

The Doctor practiced medicine in Morristown, New Jersey. He and his wife were childless. They were private people; they kept to themselves. During hunting season, he came up alone to shoot deer. His wife passed away ten years before him. He still came up to Dustin to hunt, then retired to St. Petersburg, Florida, where he had just died of a heart attack.

In the luncheonette Viola and I went over the Doctor's estate daily, deciding who would get what. We gave the plate collection to Glorine's mother-in-law. The Depression glass went to Jean Dean, the town clerk. The assessor's widow got the salt-and-pepper-shaker collection. All of them snubbed us, and we thought about giving these things to strangers instead, but the temptation to round out their collections, thus raising the overall prestige of the hamlet, proved irresistible.

The *National Geographic*s went to Viola—only one issue was missing since 1918. In Glorine's absence, we gave her the maple bunk beds with matching bureaus. She was abstaining from the luncheonette these days in accordance with the terms of the loan she received from Thea. There were lines and lines of precious antiques. We wanted Henry to have them, though he aspired only to come away with a few old tools. He warned us that certain items in this ad would draw dealers from all over the East Coast:

museum-quality Shaker table, mission furniture from Albany railroad station (needs restoring); rhino horn & velvet conversation-piece chair.

The bear rug went to Detering. The Leicas went to me. *Nearly new Leicas, lenses, tripod, accessories, view by appointment,* read the description. *Nearly new* was an understatement. The Leicas had never been used. I had viewed them by appointment behind the locked doors of the law office's walnut-paneled conference room. Boz was the attorney handling the estate. To discourage interest, he omitted from the ad the words *35mm cameras.* We were both hoping people wouldn't know what Leicas were: the world's finest single-lens-reflex 35 millimeter camera. The *Camera 35 Magazine Price Guide* rated the Doctor's models as worth three to four thousand dollars, depending on condition. These were pristine, two camera backs and three mint-condition lenses, lovingly nestled each in its own padded silk pocket in a fancy leather camera bag. As soon as I saw them, a sickening greed lunged to ugly life in the pit of my stomach.

"May I touch them?" I asked Boz politely, though I felt rude.

"Please do."

The weight of the lens in my hand, the sudden, solid way it locked into the body, its quiet sheen, the exquisite precision of the shutter—these attributes invaded me. I examined the lenses—no scratches; explored the side pockets—filters, flash attachment, self-timer; frisked the back compartment—a folding tripod. I felt barbaric and homicidal; I empathized with my ancestors, Vikings in open boats who looted their way up and down the North Atlantic for centuries.

Never had a man offered me an object I really, really wanted. I was so grateful, I was hyperventilating. Boz returned the leather bag to the vault. He closed the heavy door and gave the combination lock a twirl. When he turned to face me again, I sank down onto my knees. "My God," he said. "Thank you."

Auction day dawned misty and frail. Even down on the crossroads, I could hear the promising ring of hammers—the auction crew setting up the great white tent. I walked up the hill to the Doctor's house early. Men were unloading folding chairs from a truck and setting them up in rows under the tent. The light over the Doctor's hayfields was pink and gold. The air was fragile and moist. There was a hint of blue sky to come as the mist began to burn off.

The Doctor's house did not look happy. Its worst nightmare had come true: strangers had swarmed in, rifled through its owner's private treasures in a noisy, mercenary hubbub, and reduced his life to dollar signs. The open gritted teeth of the front stone steps were clenched in impotent despair.

A collective sense of embarrassment and exposure exuded from the Doctor's things. The bear rug was draped over the veranda railing headfirst, as if submitting to a hazing ritual. The stag heads were clustered on the lawn mount-side down, noses skyward, as if a migrating herd from another dimension had gotten stuck. The Doctor's fine display cabinets, each filled with costly glassware or fragile china, seemed poised for a nervous breakdown. His beautiful Aubusson, the Adirondack stick chairs, his fancy English lamps, an array of timid oil paintings in aggressive gold frames— everything seemed to shudder at being dislodged from its rightful place in the dark stone house. Only the guns maintained their menacing air—there were three racks, all with Day-Glo orange cardboard tags dangling from the triggers, marked with large, clear, take-me-home serial numbers.

Henry was right: the dealers began to arrive in big vans

equipped with roof racks and bearing Virginia, Pennsylvania, and Massachusetts license plates. Most knew one another. They socialized warily, smoking cigarettes and sipping coffee.

By eight, there was a steady hum of engines as people parked their cars in the fallow hayfield. The line to register for a bidder's card extended down the Doctor's driveway and out onto the road. I flirted with the auctioneer's assistant enough to find out when the Leicas were slated to come up. His docket had the small furniture at eleven, the Leicas at noon, then a break for lunch.

The buyers formed clear constituencies. The amateur collectors were nicely dressed ladies who came in pairs. Mothers with children had more practical sights; they milled about the driveway, testing the mattresses on the Doctor's beds, trying the drawers in the bureaus. The men gravitated toward the guns. There was that sound: *Winchester, Winchester, Winchester.*

Viola was all dolled up in something new and yellow, going for the *Geographic* look, I guess. The residents of Dustin who would have nothing to do with one another down on the crossroads huddled together in the tall grass with the air of a defective minority transported here from a county facility. Only Rocky and Helen of the State Farm Insurance agency circulated. Chain-smoking and sharing a cane, they criticized any item they encountered. "Looka that crack. We got one in better shape than that."

The auctioneer pounded the gavel. The assistant handed him lot no. 1—mason jars, cigar boxes, and bric-a-brac. I took my seat in the second row and gripped my card—number nine. The auction began. The china and the glassware went piece by piece to the dealers. It pained the lady collectors, but they were forced to drop out of the bidding every time. The antique furniture followed the same pattern. The deer heads and the bear rug were also out of reach of the amateurs. A very tan, cruelly calm man from Lake George who was opening a resort took every hunting and fishing trophy. He took the guns, too, almost without exception. He was rich and well prepared. Boz had informed me that only one other person, a male, had been in to view the Leicas. It had to be him.

As the auctioneer brought up the lesser furniture, I began to clear my throat. The prices went sky-high—everyone wanted furniture—and that made it take longer. At 12:30, instead of bringing up the Leicas, they broke for lunch. People vacated their seats and moved around the auction grounds. I sat on the edge of the folding chair, my hand fused to my number nine card, rigid with adrenaline, afraid that if I left my seat, I'd never find it again.

The sun was warm. The sky was almost white. People straggled back to their seats, reeking of hot dogs, onions, and mustard. At 1:30 the auctioneer took a last drag on his cigarette. His assistant shouldered the Doctor's lovely leather bag, idly stroking the inventory tag. I looked around for the tan man. He was not yet in his seat. I felt faint. I felt sick. I felt shrill and off-key. The gavel sounded.

In glowing detail, the auctioneer described the bag and its contents, three times. *Nothing less than the world's best 35 millimeter cameras . . . single-lens-reflex . . . lenses ground in Germany . . . last a lifetime . . . only 35 millimeter camera with guaranteed resale value.* He launched the chant, the undulating, sonorous, anxiety-producing, perspective-annihilating chant, looking for the opening minimum bid. I raised my card.

"Two hundred, I got two hundred, two hundred from the little lady in the shorts right here in the front row." I wished he hadn't said *little lady* or *shorts.* He made me sound like someone who shouldn't own the world's finest cameras, whose destiny was to be squashed, manipulated, denied her heart's desire.

He repeated himself, extolling the cameras with phrases that were so private, so important to me, that to hear them encanted out loud again and again seemed a sacrilege. His voice circled the faces under the tent, then widened the hunt to the perimeter, smoothly, patiently, amorally like a vulture, appealing to predators of any species.

The young photographer from the local paper took the bait, upping the ante fifty dollars at a time. Sweat poured down my arms, out of my palms, down the backs of my legs. Two men working together to take what I wanted most—I almost let it get to me. But Boz was on my side. And so, I imagined, was the Doctor, smiling that careful, ambiguous, intelligent smile. He wasn't really a Dustin man and I wasn't really a Dustin woman.

The photographer bid. I bid. We repeated ourselves. When it was his turn to offer five hundred dollars, he got nervous. He dropped out.

The auctioneer tried to keep him in the bidding. His tone assailed the fellow, his eyes belittled him. Now it was his turn to sweat. Finally the auctioneer let him go. The Leicas went once, twice, they went to me. The gavel sounded.

Glorine let out an Appalachian holler. Viola applauded. Henry fired me a remote, accusing stare. I hadn't mentioned the Leicas to him. If he knew I had five hundred dollars to spend, he would have found something worth less to sell me himself.

The door on the Porta-John down by the garage opened. There came the tan man up the driveway, tightening his belt after a bout with something—for whatever it was, I was grateful.

At four P.M. the last item went to the last bidder. We all trailed out to our cars in the hayfield. The auction crew broke down the tent. The Doctor's furniture rode out of Dustin tied ignobly to the roofs of autos, roped and hoisted into out-of-state vans. His fine china was wrapped in recent *Wickley Citizens* and professionally packed. His lesser things—lamps, bric-a-brac, and curios—rode to their new homes on individual laps. The guns and the hunting trophies were dispatched to a truck by employees of the tan man.

I led the Dustinites down the hill. The little lady in shorts was the only one taking something of value back to the hamlet. Behind me trailed the ragtag single-file disenfranchised dribble of humanity that populated the crossroads. Bringing up the rear was Fran Mrzoz. On her shoulder was a hundred-foot roll of red snow fence. She had bid a dollar.

I spread the Leicas out on my kitchen table to list the serial numbers for my insurance. Tucked away in a corner in its own silk pocket was a silver film canister. I shook it. There was something inside: negatives. I stood at the window, unfurling the film. The Doctor had shot portraits of his wife dressed for church. This made no sense. She'd been dead ten years. The cameras were new. I continued unfurling the film. It had to be her. I'd seen the hat and gloves in the clothing bin at the auction. She was standing in front of a white wrought-iron plant stand—I'd seen that there, too. She was a big woman, a prissy woman, holding her purse awkwardly, as if she didn't know what to do with it. Yes, it looked as if the whole roll was her.

Halfway through, she began to ham it up. She tossed the purse aside, then, frame by frame, she began to do cheesecake, first with her hands on her hips, then on her knees, then cupping her huge bazooms. Eventually, she stepped out of her dress altogether and posed in her corset. Her lips were pursed, sex kitten–style. Her neck and throat were thick and square. Her forearms were hairy. Her bazooms were balloons. She was the Doctor.

Outside in back of our stores, Henry was burning garbage. In and out of the shop he went, carrying boxes of useless detritus out to the fifty-gallon oil drum. Whatever he was burning now had the toxic rubbery smell of smoldering tires. The vapors rising out of the trash gave the Dustin swamp the wavy look of a movie flashback.

There had to be some honor among perverts. As soon as Henry went inside for the next box of junk, I slipped out and dropped the Doctor's negatives into the fire. They crackled and popped. I watched them melt. I could feel the Doctor's things, on their way to Lake George, heave a collective sigh of relief in the back of the rich man's van, blessing me for my complicity and wishing me years of success with the Leicas.

Viola

The CLOSED sign was posted in the window of the Dustin luncheonette on and off during April while Viola prepared her remarks to the Minisink County Historical Society. Her silhouette was visible night and day at the counter, her long, black hair held off her face by a fake leopard-skin headband, her pencil poised over an open spiral binder. I stayed away out of respect.

Viola had been to junior college. She'd wanted to teach history. There should have been time to pursue higher education—Viola could not have children—but she was enlisted to care for her husband's ailing mother. The old woman was expected to die within a year. One year became ten. When she did die, and Bud inherited the luncheonette, Viola was drafted to run it. She did it her way, serving nothing but coffee and the *New York Times*. "I am not," she said, "cooking bacon for strangers."

So as not to distract Viola, I drove to Wickley for coffee in the morning; I tiptoed past the luncheonette window for my walk at night. I had offered to help Viola. With a week to go before her presentation, she called. She needed to rehearse.

The luncheonette was cold inside, the kind of hollow, unremitting cold that narrows a room and darkens it. Over her bright red stretch pants, Viola wore her striped woven poncho, like Clint Eastwood's in *A Fistful of Dollars*. At her feet was an electric heater so small and old, it looked and sounded like a toy. I sat at the counter beside her. No steam rose from her coffee cup. It was filled with red wine.

"This is a work-in-progress," she said.

"No problem."

"It needs—polishing," she said.

"Fine."

"I don't take criticism well," she said.

I reassured her, patting her hand. Her fingers were ice-cold, the nails savagely unkempt.

She arranged her notes. She brushed back her hair. She cleared her throat. Holding the page before her as if she were about to sing, she raised her eyebrows, established eye contact. "My topic this evening," she said, "is early religious life in Minisink County." I smiled approval prematurely.

"The first church in Minisink County was the Dutch Reformed church." Her voice grew softer and more insecure with each word. "It was built of wood in the town of Freshkill in 1732. The second church in Minisink County was the Methodist church built in Newbury in 1750. It was also built of wood. The third church was also built of wood. It was the Presbyterian church built in Wickley in 1788 of wood."

Viola put down the binder.

I was speechless.

She was looking at me insolently, her arms folded across her chest, her chin cocked at the drunk's aggressive angle. I tried to get my bearings. "It . . . needs . . . research," I said.

"I have never been so insulted in my life," Viola said. "If that's all you can say to me, dear heart, then I say this to you." Viola ripped the page out of the binder and tore it in half down the middle. She let the pieces flutter to the floor. "You made me do that," she said. She poured more red wine into her cup.

We tried again the following afternoon. I was in the darkroom working on the hospital job. The hospital job was my big break, or so I was told frequently by the members of the board. My photographs of hundreds of painful, expensive, white machines would fill the new fund-raising report. I would get a credit. Wealthy donors throughout the region would see my name. I was as grateful as I could be, given the tedium. Four weeks in the darkroom with medical machines was the photographer's equivalent of self-flagellation. The phone rang.

"Are you going to help with the research or not?" Viola said. Her tone was bossy and obligating. I finished up the MRI and walked across the highway.

Viola's newspaper collection, several hundred *Wickley Citizens* dating back to 1914, was stacked against the rear wall. We divided the stack roughly in half and went through the papers, looking for anecdotes.

"Peace with the Indians was followed by epidemics," Viola read aloud. "Influenza ravaged the populace of Wickley, followed by scarlet fever. Eleven infants died in January alone."

"Here's something about *religion*," I said. Viola was leaving it up to me to point her toward her topic. "A spire was erected on the

Baptist church in Slagtown," I said. It was the church where the Historical Society met. "Solid stone, rising to a height of a hundred and eighty-six feet from the ground."

Viola snaked the paper out of my grasp and copied the item down word for word.

"And look what I found," she said. She tapped somberly on a tiny engraved illustration in a display ad. "Spurs were fifteen cents!"

That evening I spotted an amusing exchange of editorials over the winter of '21 between the stove and anti-stove Baptists. On freezing Sundays, when the congregants were required to sit through two long services in the unheated church, the anti-stove faction proposed that it was sinful to enter the tavern across the road between services to warm up at the potbellied stove.

"If only I had known you from the beginning," Viola said. "How different my life would be today." Her eyes teared up. Her face moved so close to mine that I thought she'd fall off the stool. "You," Viola said, "are my moral support."

When I left, I had met my quota for the day: I'd gone through a third of my stack. Viola was still on page fifteen of paper number one.

I spent the next morning in the darkroom, to give Viola time to catch up. I was printing Obstetrics. It was the one happy part of the hospital, to everyone except me. Boz's wife was expecting her baby any day. I wanted to do Obstetrics quickly and get it over with, but I kept rushing the prints, making the same error in timing over and over again, lifting the group photo of the cesarean team out of the tray with my tongs before its time, so that the facial expressions of the young doctors were ghoulish and satanic and had not yet reached their rightful, jubilant, full-term charisma.

I walked across the highway to see how Viola was doing. She was listing to starboard on the stool. She hadn't started reading papers yet. "Every woman in that Historical Society is an educated woman," she said. "And not one of them has to live with what I have to live with." She told me again about the error she'd made. Bud was a Future Farmer of America. She was the high school beauty queen. She could have had anybody. The boy she liked two-timed her. On the rebound, she married Bud.

She repeated herself, as drunks do. I stopped listening and thumbed through *Citizens*. On May 22, 1922, a scandal was revealed at the Baptist church. A minister was removed for incarcerating his daughter in the belfry for twelve years. I handed her the headlines. "Bingo," I said.

"I'll thank you to keep that to yourself," Viola said. "It just so happens to involve someone related to our president."

"Our president," I said. I was picturing the White House.

"Madeline," Viola said.

Madeline Davis, president of the Historical Society, had married into a family of wealthy paranoids. Viola first encountered the Davis scandal in her research several years ago.

"The girl was ahead of her time," Viola said. "She wanted to climb trees and wear pants. She liked to shoot squirrels. The reverend ordered her to stop these practices. When she didn't, he locked her in the bell tower. He rigged up the bell rope so he could sit at the desk in his study and pull the rope if his daughter so much as made a peep. The ringing drowned out the sound of her cries. She ended up in the insane asylum."

"That's good," I said. "That's interesting."

"Madeline said no," Viola said. "Actually, *she* didn't. Her friend Jenna did. Jenna called me up and told me in no uncertain terms to lay off. She said Madeline didn't want to be blamed for dredging up dirt on Davises."

"She's the president and she couldn't tell you herself?" I said.

"Madeline is very dignified," Viola said. "Her husband has her followed. His mother thinks Madeline is out to get her! You," Viola said gravely, "have no idea."

I did have an idea. I had more of an idea than I wanted her to know. I went behind the counter and found a coffee cup. I poured us both some wine.

We read all afternoon and into the night. Viola found an interesting disclaimer regarding a rigged horse auction. I found an ambitious piano recital program presented by students ages nine through twelve of Miss Antonia Ogilvie. I finished my stack and started on hers.

Saturday morning I had a headache. I sat with Henry on the bench outside his store, drinking coffee and trying to wake up. Across the highway Viola's husband, Bud, backed up their rusted-out yellow Cadillac to the luncheonette door. Bud was a tall, fair fellow, genial and warmhearted. He worked long hours on their turkey farm. In his spare time, he invented machines. He thought the world of Viola, even after the incident with Roman, and would do anything for her. I watched in horror as Bud began to unload hundreds and hundreds of newspapers. I had made a big mistake, helping Viola with her stack last night. I went into the darkroom to hide.

I printed the oncology wing. I was just waiting for Viola to call so I could give her a piece of my mind. I printed the rehab center. It was outdated. I was asked to make it look as dark and clunky as possible. At noon, when I hadn't heard from Viola, I walked across the highway to the luncheonette to see what was going on.

❖ 151 ❖

"Where have you been?" she said. She waved at the new bunker of old papers. "You've only got two days left to weed out the gems."

"Me," I said. "What about you?"

"I'm depressed," she said.

"Viola," I said. "Postpone."

"I've already done that," she said. "Twice."

"Good, then you know how."

Viola moved closer, trying to ensnare me with her abject neediness. "These are educated women, Tamara. They are expecting something scholarly. And not one of them has to live with what I have to live with."

"Postpone," I said, and walked toward the door.

"I'll kill myself," she called after me. The single overhead fluorescent bulb winced on cue. I winced, too.

I did Cardiology. I did Proctology. I took my walk, tiptoeing past the luncheonette window. Viola was at the counter, listing portside, pen poised over the open binder. I cooked chili. I watched the sun go down over the hill. Finally I couldn't stand it any longer. Was Boz a father yet? I drove to Wickley looking for his red car. He wasn't at home. He wasn't at work. No, not yet—he was at the bar.

When I got home, the answering machine was bleating silently with red, red love. It was Boz. He wanted to see me.

After supper there was a knock on the door. Under her poncho, Viola tilted and weaved. It was an arresting gravity-defying spectacle. "I smelled chili," she said. I fed her. She told me she'd unearthed some good material, no thanks to me. She asked me to clock her.

She shuffled through her pages, cleared her throat, and smiled. "Good evening," she said in a cultivated tone. "And welcome owl."

I laughed.

"You're just waiting for me to flub my lines," she said. "Good evening. And welcome *all*." She made the *so there* face. "The subject of my talk this evening is early religious life in Minisink County." She put down that page and looked for the next one. "This use of stone was a first . . . no." She shuffled and reshuffled.

"After peace was achieved with the Lenni Lenape Indians, the early pioneers were free to pursue their strongly held religious convictions. They were so staunch and firm in their faith that long before their numbers were sufficient to incorporate a congregation, many would assemble in crude buildings to hear the preaching of itinerant clergymen. It would be years before the people would convene in a house of worship as spacious and majestic as the church in which we gather tonight. The church in which we gather tonight was built of rough-cut blue limestone carried from the quarry in Milledgeville. A spire of solid stone rising to a height of a hundred and eighty-six feet from the ground was erected twenty-five years later. This use of stone was a first in Minisink County. Previous churches had to a large extent been built of wood.

"The first church in Minisink County was the Dutch Reformed church. It was built of wood in the town of Freshkill in 1732. The second church in Minisink County was the Methodist church built in Newbury in 1750. It was also built of wood—"

"Stop," I said. "Get rid of the 'churches made of wood.' Go to the next anecdote."

"That's all I have," Viola said.

I showed her the stopwatch. I handed her the phone. "Call Madeline," I said. "Tell her without the belfry, the talk is two minutes long."

She pouted. She picked up the receiver. She dialed. Her lips quivered. She looked at me. I knew what was coming next. The line was ringing. "Could you?" she said, and handed the receiver to me.

A man said hello. I hung up, surprising myself and justifying his paranoia. I had to fortify myself for this. I opened a bottle of wine and poured a glass.

Viola raised her eyebrows. "You have been drinking a lot more lately," she said, and poured some for herself.

This time when the man answered, I asked crisply for Madeline. He stayed on the line while I introduced myself as Viola's research assistant. There was a silence during which Madeline and I both listened to her husband breathing. I was calling, I said, because there was a problem with Viola's topic. Madeline cut me off.

"Could we speak face-to-face," she said. "Tomorrow perhaps?" We agreed to meet at four.

"If only I had known you from the beginning," Viola said to me. "How different my life would be. You. Truly. Are my moral support."

It rained all night and all the next day. I met Boz at noon at the St. Francis Cemetery. There were six or seven family mausoleums in the old section—great, ornate, mossy, moldy, cold, competitive, columned things. Behind them, a statuesque row of larch trees obscured a service road. I got there first and waited with the heater going and the radio on. The windshield wipers slapped the rain away right and left. Boz came. We got in his car and did things. We did what lovers do at the end; we ruined what we had so we wouldn't miss it as much. Then we both went home.

The light on the answering machine was flashing. It was Jenna,

urging me in a clipped, tight, vicious voice to back off and stop stirring up trouble where I don't belong.

Madeline lived in a magnificent polished stone manor. She was also polished and magnificent. Her eyes had the quickness and confidence of the high-IQ, straight-A student. Her skin was youthful and firm in the unnatural way I associated with hormone treatments. "I have heard so much about you," I said, stepping in out of the rain and offering a hand to shake.

She visibly braced for our physical contact. "Probably too much for my taste," she said. She offered me a wing chair by the fire and sat opposite me in its mate.

"What's the problem," she said. Her manner was public and stiff.

"We need to postpone," I said.

"I'm not happy with this," she said. "Not happy at all. Viola had three years to research this topic."

I wondered if we were being monitored. I did something I wished people had been bold enough to do for me in such circumstances. In sign language, I asked her if the nut jobs were eavesdropping. I made the cuckoo sign, spiraling the tip of my index finger at my temple, then pointed upstairs, downstairs, in the next room, my eyes furnishing the question marks.

Her breath caught in her throat. She nodded furtively yes. She pointed to the room behind us.

I proceeded carefully, using her language as I understood it. "Viola is slow," I said, "and for someone with a performance phobia, this is a particularly narrow topic."

"You couldn't find anything?" she said, maintaining her position of total impatience.

"We have two minutes," I said.

"That's ridiculous," she said. The pitch of her dismissiveness was perfect. "If we postpone another year, she'll wait until the last minute and come up with four minutes."

"That's a distinct possibility," I said, as if conceding.

"What do you recommend?" she asked. She made her voice sound as if she were putting me on the spot. Privately, she regarded me with suspicion.

"If you consent to our broadening the field of research," I said. "We might have another half an hour." I was making her nervous now.

"It would have to be—good research," she said, almost giving us away. "Nothing sensational—or spurious."

"Of course," I said. "We *are* historians. We would only admit *history*." Now I was putting her on the spot. We were head-to-head now.

"What'd you find?" she asked.

"We can document gender roles in the architecture and music of the early church," I said. By *architecture,* I meant *belfry.* By *music,* I meant *bells.* She knew what I meant.

She shook her head at me, no, no, no. I let her twitch a bit in her wing chair. "That," she said, "has nothing to do with religious life."

"So we'll go with the two minutes."

"Yes, you will," she said. She was furious.

She stood up. I stood up. She followed me to the foyer. As I put on my raincoat, I looked at the framed portrait of the Davis family reunion hanging on the wall. There were many proud, stern men. There were women with sideways smiles and dead eyes. Madeline opened the front door for me. I stepped outside.

It was raining in sheets. I took advantage of the privacy afforded by the sound of the storm to confide. "Look," I said, "I'm sorry. I know what you were up against in there." The expression on her face told me she wanted to be rid of me, the sooner the better. I was getting wet. She was dry. "My mother was mentally ill," I said.

Madeline's intelligence lunged at me as if to catch me in midfall. "Oh, my God," she said. Then she said, "*Was? She got better?*"

"No, she killed herself," I said. I had her full, knowledgeable compassion. It felt good. "She took my dad and sister with her. She set the house on fire."

"You dear," she said.

"Don't tell Viola. I'd just as soon no one around here know."

Halfway back to Dustin, a car began to tailgate me, flashing its brights. It had to be Boz. I pulled onto the shoulder and stopped. The rain splashed in on my face as I rolled down my window. It wasn't the red Mercury that pulled up alongside me. It was a new silver Lincoln Town Car. The passenger window hummed as it recessed into the padded wine-colored leather of the car door. It was Madeline. "God damn it," she said. "Put it in. Put it *all* in." She handed me something in a plastic bag and drove away.

Viola was waiting. We opened it together. It was a dusty red leather diary with a cracked binding. *Day Book* read the fancy calligraphy on the flyleaf. *Ona Monica Davis, Otisville Asylum, July 16, 1918.*

"What on earth did you say to her?" Viola said.

We stayed up until four A.M., flagging passages in the diary that would enhance Viola's talk. We were both impressed with the originality of Ona's observations, the odd poetry of her writing style, her compassion and generosity. In the back of the diary was a touching record of butterflies sighted: genus, hour, day, year, location on the asylum grounds.

We agreed to rehearse in the morning. I walked over to the luncheonette at nine. It was dark. At noon, when I still hadn't heard from Viola, I called her at home. Bud picked up.

"Viola's sick abed," he said.

I drove out to their farm. Bud was designing an incubator on the dining-room table. A complex layer of family clothing covered most of the living-room floor. Bud loped over to the stairs to announce my ascent. "That girl's coming up," he whooped.

The air in the bedroom was close and stale. Viola lay in bed under mounds of coverlets. Her black hair spilled wild and uncombed over the pillow. There were blue bags under her eyes.

"Did you call the doctor?" I said.

"I'm not *sick* sick," Viola said. "I'm upset."

"You'll do fine," I said.

"It's not that."

"What is it, then?" I asked.

"I have nothing to wear," Viola said.

There was one blouse in particular that she wanted, white polyester with ruffles at the throat. She always wore it with her black velvet blazer. "Everyone compliments it," she said.

I looked for it in her closet, in Bud's closet, and on the living-room floor. All I could find that was white was a soiled dress shirt of Bud's. We appropriated it for Viola. Together we took it "down cellar" to the washing machine. Viola opened the lid. She screamed. There was *the* ruffled white blouse. She'd started to wash it a month before, but the washer broke. Bud had been meaning to fix it.

SERIOUSLY

"No one," she said, "in that Historical Society has to live with this."

We drove to the Laundromat in Wickley. With each approaching mile, I grew more agitated. "This is not the turn," Viola said as I took the right onto West Street. Boz's red car was not in his driveway. I turned left onto Main, passing his office. No red car. "You missed it," Viola said. I drove through the parking lot of the bar—nothing.

"Take a right," Viola said.

I turned left and gunned the engine, just making it through the intersection as the stoplight turned yellow. Already I could see it in back of St. Mary's Community Hospital, the red Mercury, parked at the emergency entrance at what could only be called an emergency angle.

"This is not it," Viola said. "This is the hospital."

We washed the blouse. Viola lifted it out of the machine and shook it. The wet polyester shone like silk. Holding it up by the shoulders, she turned to me. "Can you iron?" she whined.

I was chain-smoking nervously on the edge of the bench. I looked hard at Viola, the abusive victim. My next thought surprised me: I need a *real* friend. "Throw the goddamn thing in the dryer," I said.

I was the last to arrive at the Slagtown Baptist Church that evening. The flyer announcing the talk, hand-penned in Old English by Viola, was thumbtacked to the door. I pried the massive, creaking door open—it took both hands. It was colder inside the old stone church than outside. The smells of the vestibule— waxed linoleum, candles, the cheap ink of the church publications in the literature rack, coffee percolating in an industrial-size aluminum urn—were nostalgic to me, the midwestern smell of useless good intentions.

Six well-heeled women stood about the vestibule, sipping from steaming cups. Then there was Viola. I felt a pang on her behalf— her apparel identified her as poor. She'd found a cameo brooch for the throat of her ruffled blouse. Her black velvet blazer was threadbare at the elbows and tight as a screech under the arms. Below the waist Viola had not addressed the formality of this occasion at all—she was her usual self in bright red stretch pants.

"Everyone," Viola said as I approached. "This is Tamara. My moral support." She introduced the society members in turn, pronouncing each name as if it were a solid stepping-stone in fast, dangerous waters. "This is *Ruth*. This is *Mildred*. This is *Nan*. This is our true scholar, *Pearl*. Madeline you know. This is *Jenna*." Jenna, Madeline's sidekick, was tallish and nondescript with long shaggy bangs that obscured her expression. She twisted away when we were introduced; she would not look at or touch me. "That's the one shoulda minded her own business," Jenna said to the others.

"Shall we?" Madeline said, her eyes meeting each of our eyes in turn.

The sanctuary was even colder than the vestibule. As we moved single file down the aisle, we donned our coats. We huddled together in the first pew. Viola assumed the lectern. She cleared her throat. She poured and drank a tall glass of water. She began to sweat.

"Good evening," she said. "And welcome all. The subject of my talk this evening is early religious life in Minisink County. Early religious life in Minisink County was relatively uneventful." The soft patter of ironic laughter echoed. I began to sweat, too.

Viola lost her place and her confidence. She drank more water. She shuffled through her papers, found the part about the itinerant clergymen, and read it straight through.

She breathed easier when she got to the rough-cut blue limestone carried from Milledgeville, and completely recovered her poise on the phrase *as the church in which we gather tonight.* She was so relieved, she used the phrase again quickly twice in connection with the solid stone spire and with the stove/anti-stove controversy of the winter of '21. She took a deep breath.

"Over seventy years ago," Viola said, her voice cracking. I glanced down the pew. Jenna held Madeline's arm rigidly in hers, as if to help brace her for fatal news. "A most ignominious incident occurred here." Madeline stiffened. Jenna blinked repeatedly at Viola, thrusting her chin forward in a martial attitude, as if standing up to her worst enemy.

"The Reverend Seth Davis punished his only child, a girl of thirteen, by imprisoning her in *that bell tower,*" Viola said. Her lips curled in fury and she pointed a strong witchy finger at the tower directly over her head. We all looked up. The wood grain went at right angles to the rest of the ceiling where Reverend Davis had built a trapdoor for the bell rope. Viola's voice approached the full-speed-ahead indignant mode she reserved for revolting gossip in the luncheonette. "She was said to be unmanageable. The only details we know are that she climbed trees in pants and was a good shot with a rifle. For this he confined her.

"When Ona pounded on the walls or cried out for help, her father rang the bell. This cruel and unusual punishment was to last twelve years until the Reverend Davis was stranded in a snowstorm far from home. The revelation came about through what is to me a most chilling turn—Ona tolled the bell herself.

"People thought it was a miracle. They flocked into the church; they climbed the stairs into the study. They unlocked the entrance to the bell tower and down she came, emaciated, ragged, and deranged.

"Records indicate that her father was not prosecuted but was invited to establish a parish in northern Ontario. Let me treat you now," Viola said, "to the words of Ona Davis herself, as I read a selection of excerpts from a journal kept over her lifetime."

Viola read too long—we had overestimated the appeal of Ona's overly poetic, King James writing style. As Viola droned on, Mildred and Nan dozed, Ruth gazed around the church, Pearl admired her own lapis lazuli pendant, Madeline tuned out. Jenna alone grew more alert, more intent with every passage Viola read. She was entranced, her attention furiously held by the incident, her chin retreating, wounded by the facts, her throat busy as she swallowed again and again, trying to force some devastating personal issue to remain lodged there where she could best deal with it.

"I close with a letter," Viola said, "written by Ona to her father's congregation. She writes and I quote, 'What sustains me in moments of painful homesickness and sorrow are the words of a high servant of the church who visited our asylum Tuesday last. He told me in a private interview that he had visited Slagtown not two weeks before and had not in any of his travels found more civil and true politeness than he met in our section of the country. He assured me that he will always remember with pleasure our beautiful valley and will cherish the names of the many inhabitants.'"

Viola lay the last page down. She awaited her due, the applause of seven educated women. It was a bit scattered in coming, but it went on at length, echoing crisply, sacrilegiously through the sanctuary.

"Thank you," Viola said, her cheeks flushing at the attention. "Thank you." I saw then the kind of a beauty Viola had been in high school: smoldering, attention-hungry, voluptuous, regal.

The dessert was Madeline's spice cake, frosted with maple walnut icing and topped with candied walnuts. It was so light, pieces kept falling off our forks and breaking into crumbs on the waxed floor. Madeline nervously scooped up the particles, expressing concern that the mess might attract mice. The rest of us stood together in a circle, eating cake and discussing Seth Davis. How did he deal with his daughter's menses? What did he give her to eat, and when? Why didn't anyone notice a peculiar pattern about his hours in the study? Wasn't the tolling of the bell either so irregular or so frequent that it caused suspicion?

After Madeline had cleaned up the floor, she joined us. She drew herself up with dignity. "That was excellent work," she said to Viola and me.

"It was good of you, Madeline, to yield," Ruth said. "And still to come and sit through it."

"It hasn't been easy," Madeline admitted.

Someone was missing. "Where's Jenna?" I asked.

"She's . . . *washing the coffeepot.*" Madeline said it in a tone that implied, *Leave her be.* Everyone grew silent and listened to the din. Downstairs in the church kitchen, there was a tremendous banging of aluminum—the lid, grounds basket, percolator, and urn were getting a very great scouring in the utility sink.

Someone changed the topic of conversation. I slipped away, defying Madeline one last time by descending the stairs. Jenna stood at the sink with the faucet roaring hot water. Great clouds of steam surrounded her. Her elbows jabbed violently through the vapor as she scoured and banged the aluminum pieces around and around the old sink, working her rage out with noise. Madeline was right. I left her be.

I climbed the stairs slowly, meditatively, stopping in the middle where it was darkest, recalling Boz's voice on the telephone this afternoon at 5:35, husky, exhausted, cracking with emotion, shot through with wonder, saying the three words I needed to hear to let him go forever: *It's a girl.*

Jean Dean, the Town Clerk

I had Miss Portugal under the lights. I arranged her black man-
tilla symmetrically over her hair. She was a sensuous, dark-haired
beauty with a lush emerald green taffeta skirt. I was photograph-
ing the town clerk's formidable doll collection at a discount, ten
dollars a doll. She had sixty, each dressed in the museum-accurate
national costume of a different country.

The sun was high in the sky, hours and hours from setting.
The long days, the long weeks of May were depressing. May was
my hardest month. The light was fragile; out in back, a flower-
ing tree was budding out with brave, sensual blossoms; ferns
were uncurling in the shade of the swamp. Every hopeful sign of
spring scalded me. I had no one to share my life with anymore,
and unless you counted three motel afternoons a week, never
had.

I was letting myself go, hiding the filthiness of my long hair in
a greasy French twist, wearing the same T-shirt three days running, eating potato chips for breakfast. I drove barefooted. I had

lived in Dustin for only a year, but I was starting to look as though I was born there.

Glorine was perched on a stool by the window next to me, killing time, waiting for the road crew to take their coffee break. They had roped off Route 1 next to her house and were installing a culvert. Every afternoon, she dressed up in some goofy getup as a surprise and brought them cookies. Today she wore a hot-pink halter top, matching pink capri pants that looked as if they belonged to a nine-year-old—perhaps her nine-year-old—and red spike heels. She had tried to dye her red hair platinum, but it had turned a garish Day-Glo orange. The cookie baking had not gone right, either. She mixed the batter for oatmeal raisins, but had no raisins, so threw in chunks of pink bubble gum.

"They're rock-hard," she said. "I hope Lonnie don't lose a filling." She knew the men by name. Each afternoon she asked after their families, pets, and sick relatives. The next day she would report their status to me. I envied her direct, satisfying engagement with the entire world. I was in free fall—the surfaces of my mind and body didn't seem attached. May was my month for flight. I was trying to stay put.

She lit a Pall Mall, twirling her ankle first one way, then the other, admiring her red spikes. They were from her single day of glory—she'd auditioned for a West Virginia radio talent search as a singer at sixteen and won.

"Talkin' 'bout truckers," Glorine said, though we weren't. "I woke up today wishing to God I was still married to Jerry. Wonder if Jerry ever wakes up wishing he was still married to me." A little private flicker of passion crossed her face. She must have been recalling something pleasant he did to her or she did to him.

"Probably not," she said. "Since I cut off his ear."

"His ear."

"He had it comin'. He got himself into a situation where he had two of us, a wife and a girlfriend, on the same street. And he kept stealing my stuff to take up to her place. Took me a year to find out. Six in the morning I get a telephone call from West Virginia and it's my brother telling me our mother died. I call the trucking company to find Jerry. They tell me Jerry is home with me. I call up my neighbor, Carna. Ain't that an awful name, Carna. I tell her what they told me. Glorine, honey, she says, I knowed all along, but I just didn't have the heart to tell you. He's been shacking up with Marjie Kratt right up the street for over a year now.

"There I am in my coral-colored negligee," Glorine said. "With the little scallops here." She drew a series of curlicues across her chest with patience and affection. "I take my kitchen carving knife and I walk up the street." Many of Glorine's escapades involved weapons.

"Marjie's garage door is broke and will not close all the way," Glorine said. "I peek under it. There's Jerry's car. I walk into her house, straight into her bedroom, and I stand there in my negligee, running my hand up and down the blunt side of the knife, like it really turns me on. And they're lying side by side on Marjie's yellow flowered bedsheets, cute and cozy, watching the *Today Show.* On my TV.

"Jerry's got a can of Bud in one hand," Glorine said. "Marjie's drinking coffee. All around her bedroom are things Jerry took from our house. There's my little deck of playing cards with George Jones's autographed picture on the back. There's my little set of Okefenokee Swamp coasters I bought on my honeymoon. With Jerry. There's the F volume of my *World Book Encyclopedia* on which I am paying seventeen dollars a month. And there, like I said, is my TV. My TV that disappeared a year ago when I thought Jerry was on the road and I reported it to the police as stolen.

"Marjie Kratt starts screaming, 'Jerry, honey, she's got a knife!' And Jerry, he says to her, 'She don't mean nothing by it.' And he says to me, 'Go on home, Glorine, I'll be there soon.'

"And I says to him—and my voice is just as low and cool and calm as you please—I says, 'You can bugger this fat cow every night of the week and I won't lose no sleep over it, Jerr, but you shouldn'ta taken my TV.' Marjie is running out of her house, screaming, 'Police!'

"'I'm dreadful sorry,' Jerry says, and he counts out fourteen dollars. He says, 'Here, take this toward a new one.' I put the knife blade on that crease where the ear meets the head like it's just bread and I want a slice. 'That's not enough,' I says. 'Where is Marjie's money?' 'I can't tell you that, Glorine,' he says, 'she'll kill me.'"

Glorine and I shared a long smile over that.

"She's going to kill him and there you are with the knife," I said.

"Not too bright," she said. Her eyebrows arched high and her irises got greener for emphasis. How she did that, I never found out.

"So did he hold still and take it like a man?" I said.

"He didn't have no choice. It happened real fast. It fell off his head just like that. Did you know that it's just a hole there?"

"Yes," I said, but it was the dolls I was thinking about. None of them had ears. They had a raised semicircle where the ear should be.

"Still got the ear somewheres up in one of my jewelry boxes," Glorine said. "Hate to throw it out since it's a piece of a real human."

I straightened Miss Portugal's bolero. It was made of beaded black wool, lined with green silk, trimmed with the tiniest gold piping I'd ever seen. The shadows on her face made her look as though she was grieving. I pulled the lights closer and softened the angle. I fluffed the skirt. I aligned the toes on the lovely black suede boots. Stepping back behind the tripod, I snapped.

I put Miss Portugal back in her bag and put her bag back in her box. She was especially lovely. I kind of hated to squelch her by putting the lid on, but I stopped short of doing what Jean Dean did—she never put a lid back on a doll box without saying, *Night, night,* to the doll.

Funny how different she was from her dolls. She had a mussed white bun and a black mustache. She was malodorous and slovenly. The hems of her homemade skirts dipped this way and that where they'd tried to respond to her various weight gains.

She was sneaking her dolls over to the gallery five at a time. She didn't want the other two Presbyterians in the hamlet to see her associating with me—I didn't go to church. She looked both ways to see if the coast was clear, then waddled across the highway with her great breasts lolling from side to side in a 3XXX fuchsia T-shirt that read LET'S HEAR IT FOR DOLLS. She had clumsily tried to bully me into giving her my lowest price by intimating she was big in the doll world. Her breath alone was justification for turning her down. But the dolls, the dolls. When she lifted a lid, I shivered.

I knew a break when life handed me one. I recognized the innocent childlike lifting of the spirits that came with miniatures. Dolls
would help me stay put.

"Yep," Glorine said. "Except for that stealing, old Jerry wasn't
a bad egg. I can't abide a thief."

"Glorine, I need a favor," I said. "Could you steal something for
me?"

Twice I had asked Boz for my dirty pictures. I knew where
they were: in the office in the bottom desk drawer on the left. He
kept them in an envelope labeled DUSTIN CASE. He kept telling me
he'd get them to me, but I knew he wouldn't. I wanted them back.
It was important.

"Steal, Tammy-girl?" Glorine said. She inhaled hard and gave
me that greener than green-eyed look. "For you, I'd *kill*." It was
the nicest thing any friend had ever said.

Boz did matrimonial law. We called his receptionist. Glorine
made an appointment for the next morning to discuss a possible
divorce. That night, we dyed her hair back to red. I styled it in a
flip. We found a navy dress in her closet. I gave her my matching
cultured pearls, hoping Boz wouldn't recognize them as his
Christmas present to me. "They're real," I said.

"Which president's wife do I look like," she said, sitting tall at
her vanity, turning her good side to the mirror.

"Rosalynn Carter," I said.

"I wish it was a Republican," she said.

Her appointment was at ten. I expected Glorine to be back by
noon. I had Miss Scotland under the lights. Her wavy red hair and
saucy tartan beret were high-spirited and seductive in an athletic
way. It was easy to imagine no bloomers under her kilt and a good
Scottish wind coming up. I snapped, wondering if I was losing my

mind. I put kinky Miss Scotland away. By two, I was unable to look at another doll.

I was pacing back and forth, running to the gallery window whenever an automobile entered the crossroads, even though nothing could be mistaken for Glorine's old white station wagon. It had the underpowered sound of the economy car, as if the same motor were used in blenders. Glorine got out of the car, a Pall Mall glowing red between her teeth, the pearls glowing white in the soft spring afternoon light. As she crossed the highway, her right hand kept floating up to touch the pearls. She had it. The sight of the familiar 8 x 10 manila envelope under her left arm was as sweet as anything I'd seen coming toward me in weeks.

I took the envelope. "Thank you, thank you, thank you," I said. She checked the ghost of her reflection in the window, her hand resting on the pearls.

"We talked four hours!" she said. I was jealous. He never talked to me for four hours. "I told him my whole life story," she said. "Train sex and all." I was even more jealous. It had taken me three months to get the train sex story from Glorine.

"Drink?" I asked her because I needed one.

"Coffee. If it's no trouble," she said. She sat on the stool, smoking and relishing the happiness she'd spread in the world today, helping a new person get to know her. I went into the back room and made a fresh pot. I peeked through the curtain at her, watching her smoke and twirl her ankle. Even her smoking was more First Lady–like with the pearls around her neck. She reached toward the ashtray every few moments as delicately as if she were about to pen her memoirs, tapping the ash off before it even got started.

I gave her the star treatment, china cup and saucer, sugar bowl, creamer, silver spoon—all on a tray.

"Ritzy," she said. She sipped her coffee.

I photographed Miss Bali. Of the sixty, Miss Bali was the only disappointment. Her black hair was parted American Indian–style in the middle. Because her feet didn't have toes, her shoes were slippers, not sandals. Her batik sarong didn't really fit. What she really needed was a good pair of tits.

I wondered if Glorine had inspected the contents of the envelope. Ninety-nine people out of a hundred would have immediately pulled off the road, opened it, and had a good long look. But Glorine wasn't nosy, she was grandiose. She had to be.

From the gallery window, we could see the crew gathering around the striped barricade, their flashing orange caution light pulsing like a portable civic heart. They were lighting one another's cigarettes, gabbing softly, adopting all the postures of leisure, checking their watches, waiting for their surprise.

"Wait," I said. Glorine had a Pall Mall going in the hand that rested on the pearls. I lit her face. I lit her neck. I snapped a picture.

She slid off the stool.

"You got any Lorna Doones or some such for my crew?" she asked. She'd lost her baking time, stealing for me.

"I'm afraid not," I said. All I had was a little pot, and I needed every bit of that to stay put. She reached behind her neck to unclasp the pearls.

"Keep them," I said. "You earned them."

When Glorine emerged from the gallery in the navy dress and pearls, a hush of respect fell over the crew. One of them began to applaud. They all joined in. She twirled and took a bow. Their clapping grew raucous and rhythmic. Catcalls pierced the delicate May air. How'd she do it, share herself so fully with the world? I hoped to find out.

Meanwhile, here came Jean Dean with five more dolls, looking both ways to see if the coast was clear. What a doll she would have made.

We opened Miss Brittany's box. Her starched lace headdress was a work of art.

The New Lady

I saw the new lady in her yard. To garden, she wore nice sandals, a necklace, and gold earrings. I felt shy, third-grade shy. I wanted a friend, but she was too happy for me.

I watched her painting her lawn furniture from my gallery window for a week. She and her husband were restoring. They'd done it before in Connecticut, and they were doing it here in Dustin. She had a rhythm. She worked off him. I was jealous, acid-at-the-back-of-the-throat jealous, every time I watched them work together. He climbed a ladder to take out a window. She took the hammer and handed him a screwdriver. He handed her back both screws. She went inside to answer the phone. When she came back, she brought him an ice-cold drink. She said something funny and he laughed.

All this hurt. I didn't want this going on right outside my window every day. It was the love version of conspicuous consumption. They were what my sociology teacher termed Haves. I Had Not.

Her name was Terry. I found this out first from Viola. His name was Tim. Tim and Terry Thompson from Salisbury, Connecticut, rode in from the east in a Land Rover, bringing that Connecticut happiness with them. It was unfair to everyone. I'd never been to Connecticut. I assumed it was a place where the sun always shines through the New England clouds; history is valiant and maritime; every house is a Colonial, white with black shutters; every woman is blond with blue eyes—and they never get kidnapped for it.

Tim and Terry. I imagined them as born smiling and handing each other hammers. They get A's. They go to the best university. One of them smokes pot once; the other watches and asks what it's like. All their life, their white crew socks stay white. They're white even now as they restore the Dustin Hotel, which they do themselves, together, because they enjoy it and they know how. They agree on everything. At night he makes a fire in the brick fireplace. She makes a pie. If they quarrel, he comes over to her later and says he's sorry.

I know I will have to sit here and watch this happiness multiply and divide right in front of me. She will be expecting. He will have to get his own cold drinks, his own hammers, lay his own two screws aside. She'll be less focused in her special new state, losing track of time, paging through huge wallpaper books with her left hand on her belly. She will refinish a small rocker to rock in while she nurses the baby. She will refinish it outside in the shade so that even the word *fume* doesn't reach the fetus lucky enough to be engendered by Terry and Tim.

Their Christmas card photo will be posed in front of the restored mantel, this year just the two of them with Talbot, their golden retriever. Next year a baby will join the photo, wearing a

Santa hat: Truman. He holds his head up stronger and higher than other babies his age, because his parents are from Connecticut. The year after, they add a cat. In year number four Truman wears his first bow tie; Terry holds a newborn, Tess. And then they move. The schools are terrible out here, they say, as if they alone have just discovered this. People from Connecticut are used to schools with high ceilings and sun-filled rooms. In Connecticut, children play chess by the age of seven and lacrosse by eight. They don't need to take computer classes at school—they've had their own computers since they were three. Connecticut children invest in the stock market by the age of ten. They pick out their own jewels from Harry Winston before the onset of puberty.

Will they go back to Connecticut? I ask.

Connecticut? No way. Too stuffy. Too expensive. Too suburban. No, they're going to Boston! They want to fix up a 1700s warehouse on the harbor, turn it into a mixed-use space with shops below and lofts above. They'll do it themselves, because they enjoy it and they know how. They're pioneers, after all. And I'll have to smile straight through this, babysitting for Tess and Truman, playing fetch with the new puppy they get to keep Talbot company, while the moving van fills up their driveway and takes them away. Right in front of me. And I'll be a new kind of lonely then, because I love them both by then and they love me.

It happens the day Terry walks across the highway after three weeks in town, heading straight for the gallery with a look of social concern. And I inhale hard and stub out the butt and pretend to be busy, as if I didn't see her coming. I worry the whole time she approaches: how do I look, am I clean, am I in control, will she be able to tell I'm scarred and defective and have never had a real friend before?

"We haven't met officially yet," she says, opening the door and standing just outside of it. She introduces herself. "Now," she says, "I'm afraid I desperately need a favor."

"Desperately?" I say sarcastically, then I'm immediately embarrassed. Sarcasm pushes people away.

"There's a terrible smell in that trailer," she says.

"God damn," I say. "Marshall Jim is dead." My voice is calm, just noting a local fact.

I realize from the look of horror on her face that in one short year, I've become a part of this place, which is to say, I've become strange.

We go over there together. Our first activity as strangers is so intimate in a bizarre way that it makes us friends for life, as we tell people in the years to come, whenever I visit her and they ask us, *How did you two meet?*

It's Terry's story. She tells it like this:

"I follow Tamara across the highway. We start to smell it ten feet away. It stinks like an open cesspool. We're both holding our noses. The television is on loud. The door is locked. She kicks it down with a karate kick. I'm thinking, *Karate, karate, I've got to learn karate.*

"Inside, it's a life-size time capsule from 1963. There's a portrait of John F. Kennedy on the kitchen wall. The countertop is pink Formica with silver abstract lines and specks. In the dish drainer, there are two aqua plastic cups.

"'Look, Tamara,' I say, 'the original Jell-O package!' There it is, a thirty-year-old box of lime Jell-O sitting on the counter next to an avocado electric range. The stainless-steel saucepan has the right amount of water measured in. *Marshall Jim loved Jell-O,* Tamara says. *His mother meant to make him some, but then she died.*

"'Why are these caraway seeds on the floor?' I ask her, because we're wading through three inches of them, but they're softer than caraway and some are black, not brown. *Oooh boy, are you from Connecticut!* Tamara says. *Those are mouse droppings.*

"I scream and jump up onto a chair. She goes into the living room and comes right back out. *Don't go in there, Terry,* she says. *Mice have gotten to him.* So I wait in the kitchen, standing on a chair, thinking I have made a very big mistake. Tim told me to call the Department of Health. I should have listened.

"Tamara's in the living room, talking to herself. *Jim, hon,* Tamara is saying. *I need a sheet to cover you. Now where might you keep a sheet?* She is holding her nose while she talks, so she sounds like a harelip with a bad cold. And I hear her clanging, one-handed, through clothes hangers, going through closets, opening bureau drawers and banging them shut. And all this time I'm thinking, *No face, what does it mean to have no face?*

"Then the *Galloping Gourmet* comes on the TV. He's going to prepare crab rémoulade in eggplant boats. He's stirring ketchup into the mayonnaise. He's adding chopped onions. He's mincing a green pepper, zesting a lemon, tossing in capers. It's disgusting.

"*Give me a hint, Jim,* Tamara is saying. *Your mother had to have a bedsheet somewhere.*

"All of a sudden, Tamara calls me. *Terry,* she says. *Terry, come here!* I jump down off the chair and run into the living room. Tamara is holding a three-pound coffee can filled with cash, standing there right next to a moldy white eighty-five-pound corpse in rigor mortis in a BarcaLounger with a remote frozen in his hand. I scream. The TV features a close-up of the finished rémoulade.

"*Terry, pay attention,* she says. *There's six more of these. I need you as a witness.* She leads me into the bedroom. She is opening the cans and counting the money out loud. I see Marshall Jim's mother's vintage dresses hanging there in mint condition in the closet—and they're all my size. I start thumbing through them, telling Tamara what they'd bring at the Salisbury Flea Market. We've both stopped holding our noses now. She's up to three thousand dollars. I'm up to a thousand.

"We take the money to the Wickley Humane Society. We donate it anonymously in memory of Marshall Jim's coondog, Wallace. *This is to keep alive dogs who no one adopts,* Tamara tells the woman on duty. *I want to know names and dates. Every month I want a log of food and vet expenses.* There's something wild in her voice that frightens me, something hunted and unprotected. It makes me feel overprivileged. I want—desperately, though I try not to use the word lightly around her—for her to accept me.

"'Tamara,' I say, back in the car. I try to venture respectfully onto the sore subject. 'Did you,' I say, 'once lose a dog?' She reviews her whole life, looking at the broken white line rushing at us down the middle of the highway. She feels sorry for me now, because I know so little about loss. She decides to keep it simple, wrinkling her nose with a calculated lightheartedness that puts an end to the subject, at least for now. *Twice,* she says."

Tamara

For six weeks in the fall, my photographs of the hands of the people of Dustin hung on the walls of the gallery. The show had been called important by the reviewer from the *Wickley Citizen;* life here in Dustin had been called consequential. People in the hamlet came to the gallery frequently to see their hands and show them to other people. The exception was our three displaced Presbyterians, including Jean Dean. They'd attended the opening three abreast in church gear, quickly observed that they weren't in the show, then left, three abreast, in a huff. Surely they knew enough about the mechanics of photography to admit that the subject had to be present when the shutter snapped for the image to occur. After a year in town, two of the three had yet to speak to me. Their little rejection made me smile. Nora's hurt.

My sister had helped get me here and stay here, beginning with the first month's rent, ending with the purchase of the gallery when it was almost sold out from under me. The binder, the contract, the inspection report, the mortgage application—all went flying overnight to L.A. What came back was a check. Apparently she considered our mutual experience complete. With my photographs on the wall for one more day, Nora had yet to call, write, or show.

After her car accident, we'd promised each other to stay close. But she could agree to things when she was in pieces that I couldn't hold her to whole. The brave work her body had done, knitting itself back together again, stuttering over layer upon layer of scar tissue, must have left her skin even thicker, her soul even slicker. We talked even less than before. It was a gray afternoon, warm for November. The photographs would come down at five. Boz was in the gallery with Jennie, killing time. She was six months old now, with Janice's coal-black hair and perfect bow lips. I was holding her while Boz looked at the photographs. A dark blue rental car stopped across the highway.

A man in shirtsleeves got out. The jaw looked familiar and untrustworthy. The man yelled at Tim Thompson, who was nailing floorboards onto the deck. Terry was beside him, handing him nails. The man was lost. He asked directions. Tim pointed him toward the new PO.

It took a while but there they came, Detering hobbling on his cane across the pavement, his hand crooked in the elbow of the stranger. Lunging along in their wake was Dave L. Garson. An acidy adrenaline flowed in my veins. There it was, the smell of spearmint gum. I handed Jennie to Boz and moved toward the stranger as he walked in the door. "Hello, Robbie," I said.

❖

He had been a college senior when he helped out the Watertown High School Photography Club for credit. The smell of his spearmint gum in the darkroom was appealing. All of us were crammed in there at his elbows, watching him develop film. The red light made his jaw look even stronger and handsomer than it was. He was seven years older than me at a time when those seven years made us illegal.

He was not a good idea. He was not the kind of thing that sets a girl up for a healthy romantic history. Even at the time I felt my error. He was getting away with more than I was getting away with. He had it good, loving me, better than I had it, loving him. He abused his power. He toyed with me. He couldn't resist correcting me, detail by detail, until I hurt.

"You should comb your hair like hers," he'd say, pointing to a girl in a restaurant. "You could do a few stretches a day and your waist would be more like that." Another girl, this one walking down the street in shorts.

Then there were the emotional things.

"You should be happier to see me. You should be happier about everything. You're not as much fun as you were when I first met you."

It was all an extension of the way he gave photography instruction. "This area should be lighter. Dodge it a little next time to bring out the contrast." Or, "This shot is overexposed. You should bracket every time, so you have more negative to work with."

I tried whatever he said. The more I tried, the more I disappeared. "I say these things because I care about you," he said. But the alterations he asked for were not possible, and my effort gave him no pleasure. "Try to buy boots like that girl's wearing. They're sexier than the ones you have on." He couldn't resist watching me twitch. He couldn't relinquish making me squirm. He was like a boy cutting up a worm to see if both halves moved. Perhaps he sensed the hole at the core of me and the power it might someday have over him.

Still, he had no right. It wasn't my fault that I was bred and raised and fed without love. He liked to poke at that, to prod. He liked to get out his best equipment and sound the depth of the hollowness inside me. He liked to show me that he knew how. The natural power imbalance—teacher-student, knower-innocent—was something Robbie couldn't resist exploiting. This is how men are, I told myself. This is the price a girl pays for enjoying maleness.

We'd leave right from school. I'd make up an excuse so that I wasn't expected home until very late. We'd drive fifteen miles to the small town of Grenada, South Dakota, and check in at the Holiday Inn. We'd go to the room for a while, have dinner in the lounge, then Robbie would rent an adult movie and we would start in all over again. When he drove me "home," he'd drop me off at the alley. I would walk the rest of the way, slip in the back door, and go to my room without Mom or Dad ever knowing where I'd been.

When we got me in trouble, he made it my job to take care of it. I was too young to do alone what he made me do alone. There were eight of us all told in the waiting room. Half wore wedding rings. Two of us were lying about our age. The nurse took us one at a time. I felt sad each time a woman left the waiting room. We were all frightened. There was a mood of common shame and sorrow, but no one wanted to talk. We not only didn't want to get to know one another, we never wanted to see one another again.

When it was just me waiting to be taken, I grabbed a magazine and opened it. FIFTY FRESH WINNING STARTS FOR THE YEAR

AHEAD, read the headline of the article. It was the *Woman's Day* annual roundup of readers' suggestions for how to cheer up in the new year. *Visit a church of a different faith,* suggested a woman from Georgia. *Give an affectionate nickname to a person who doesn't have one.* That was from Ohio. *Take a nap in a different place*—South Dakota. I closed the magazine. The nurse was there.

They do it by vacuuming. It hurts. The doctor spoke in non sequiturs, or perhaps I just heard everything that way. "Where does it go?" I asked, meaning the fetus.

"Tissue," he said.

"No, the fetus," I said. "Where does it go?"

"Michigan," he said.

The afternoon of the fire, we were at the Holiday Inn. Robbie had given me a ring. He said we were engaged. It was later than usual when he dropped me off, two A.M. I was still happy from our time together. He said we'd travel to Europe after I'd graduated from high school. I walked down the alley, vowing to become what he wanted me to be.

At the edge of the vacant lot, the smell hit me: sickening and sweet, charred and wet, the smell of a dead fire. I ran toward the house, but the house was gone. All that was left standing was an eroded skeleton, a window casing, a doorway. The rest of it lay strewn about the burnt ground in wet, blue-black puzzle pieces.

Orange Day-Glo emergency tape roped off the site. It was irreversible. It was over. The fire department had come and gone. The bodies were in the morgue. The dark whorling at the heart of me kicked on. I was surprised at what I felt next. I felt sprung. Instead of going to find Robbie, I fled. Everything that made him necessary was gone.

We had needed a real mother. God gave us a child instead—

brilliant, paranoid, wired for death. It was all he had available when we prayed.

We gave her disease too much space, too much time. She turned that into too much power.

I knew she was going to do it. I just didn't know I knew. The *k* was silent.

There was dread in our house for three weeks leading up to the fire. There was a shift in the emotional equilibrium, toward quietness, toward resolution. Buy two-gallon containers. Fill with gasoline. Nail windows shut. Dad was at work. We were at school.

She knew she was going to do it, too. The difference was she knew she knew. The silent *k* was roaring.

❖

Now Detering was looking back and forth from Robbie to me. He was proud of himself. "He taught you photography!" he told me. Boy, was his nose for dirt dead. In the old PO he would have sniffed something statutory in Robbie's gentle crow's-feet. He would have detained Robbie, asking those deceptively pointed questions that passed for superficial conversation. Back pain had dulled Detering, rendered him literal. He grinned the foolish grin of an old man in the dark, while my truckload of shame filled up the room, as useless as a fortune in devalued currency.

"There's a little more to it than that," Robbie said.

"Or why would you come all this way," Dave L. Garson said, helping him out.

"They were engaged," Detering told Dave.

"We knew something of the sort had gone on," Dave said. "A hot number like that one there doesn't just pop up in a backwater like this every day. Boy, was she tight-lipped! Nobody could get a word out of her. Not even him—he thought she was boinking the junkman." Dave jerked his chin at Detering.

"Wasn't a morning Henry wasn't in here drinking coffee," Detering told Robbie.

Robbie chewed his gum once. This wasn't going the way he expected it to go. He'd never been at a disadvantage with me. He had never seen me surrounded by goodwill.

Across the highway, Terry was following the stages of my unwelcome reunion. Her mind was no longer on the task at hand. Instead of issuing Tim nails one by one as needed, she alternately supplied him with an awkward handful or forgot to offer any.

Dave crowded Robbie from the side to ask a personal question in that socially unfit way of his. Their chins were an inch apart. "Did you beat her?" Dave asked. I was starting to enjoy this.

"Beat? No," Robbie said.

"You might have abused her without knowing it," Dave said. "That's what I do, so they say."

"Are you her boyfriend?" Robbie asked Dave.

"Naaah," he said. "I checked her out, but she was doing this fellow here." He jerked his chin at Boz.

Boz smiled. "How do you do," he said.

It was getting to be a bit much for Robbie.

He turned to me and said in a tone that left the others out, "Did you get my letter?"

He'd written in the summer to say he'd seen Nora's name on the credit roll of a sitcom and gotten in touch with her. Everyone back home now knew about the cause of the fire and the problems my family had had. He said he now understood why I might not have been as happy a person as he wanted me to be. Perhaps he'd even added to my unhappiness. If that was true, he was sorry. But he would never understand why I hadn't sought refuge with him, given the fact that we were engaged.

He said he'd been married and divorced. His wife took their child. Part of the problem, he said, was he had unfinished business with me. Could he please hear from me? To cut him off like that was unfair. I was the love of his life, he said. He hoped I would call this number and arrange to meet him in some mutually agreeable place so we could talk. I threw the letter away.

Detering would remember a South Dakota postmark. Robbie would already have confirmed the arrival of the letter with him.

"Ask Detering," I said.

"Your handwriting is terrible, son," Detering said to Robbie.

"I never received the courtesy of a reply," Robbie said.

"There is no answer," I said.

"Everyone deserves the courtesy of a reply," Robbie said. He slid both hands in his pants pockets and looked around the room. He chewed his gum once on the right side of his mouth. He went to Plan B. "I'd like to get my ring back then," he said.

It was a thin gold band with three small diamond chips embedded in it. I had removed it on the bus to Chicago the night of the fire, placing it in the net pocket on the seat back in front of me, hoping someone who needed a very small miracle would find and pawn it.

"It's long gone," I said.

"That was fourteen-karat gold," he said. "There were three diamonds on that ring."

I kept quiet about their being chips. He described the ring in detail to the men. They allowed this, empathizing, with no twinges of competitiveness. Men from the Midwest they naively considered less male, as if the sperm between Indiana and

Montana had been diluted with excessive politeness and caution. Robbie began to brag about how much I loved him, how there was nothing he couldn't get me to do for him. "She was young, you know," he said. "You have to get 'em young." I kept quiet.

He had actually offended Detering and Dave, and now he began to bore them, citing examples of couples in Watertown who were still together and couples who were divorced. Their eyes wandered, their chins nodded vacantly, they jingled the change in their pockets. Talking at people until they yawned was part of Robbie's manipulation. He feigned dullness to regain control.

Jennie began to cry. The men took the opportunity to head for the door. Robbie finished his story, talking to the empty air where the men had recently stood. Dave L. Garson came back over and offered Robbie an insider's tour of the hamlet, trying to get him away from me. Had Dave promised to include the ten best back doors for sexual harassment, Robbie might have accepted. But he declined, saying there was no reason to stick around if he couldn't get what he'd come for. "Good luck," he said to me. He made it sound final, and that put me on edge. With Robbie, there was always a zinger.

Across the highway, Tim was on his own with the nails. Terry was standing in her loyal, attentive way at the edge of the pavement, facing the gallery, waiting for a signal in case I needed her.

Robbie walked to the door. I followed him outside.

"You're twenty-nine now?" he asked, hesitating with his hand on the knob. He had always forgotten my birthday.

"Thirty," I said.

"Watch out," he said. "That's about when we figure your mom started losing her mind."

There it went, the probe, sounding the depth, scraping the diameter of the old hollowness inside. I flinched and fell back a step. His mouth remained straight, but in his eyes I could see a grin. He had always been at ease with malice.

Terry didn't like what she saw. She walked over and told Robbie to get the hell out of town. Tim backed her up, standing by Robbie's blue rental car with the hammer until Robbie got in and drove away.

I walked Boz and Jennie out to their car.

Back inside, I looked at my photographs as if I were Nora. They were alien. They were jarring. They were black-and-white, breaking the first rule of entertainment. They were wise, breaking the first two rules of family: once a failure, always a failure, and failures are not allowed wisdom. The knowledge in these was deep and sure. The silent *k* was talking:

Bachelor

HENRY STOREY, OWNER OF ODDS 'N ENDS ANTIQUES

The hands look rustic and complete, the left folded loosely over the right, palms down, as if at the end of a self-reliant day. No ring, of course. You should be done looking, but your eyes detect a puzzle. You count. He doesn't add up. One hand starts out with four fingers and tapers up to three. Why or how you'll never know. He'll never tell. Neither will she.

Uncivil Servant

STANLEY DETERING, POSTMASTER

See this fist? It's for you. All those lines are paper cuts, issued at the rate of two hundred a year, always when a person least expects them. The sorter's callus on this thumb could do first-class by nine, second-class by ten, bulk by noon, and junk the same day (though three days are allowed), if it weren't stopping every two seconds to sell a stamp to you. One stamp. You can't buy a hundred? Fifty? How about twenty? Can you buy ten? No, you have to stop me from doing my job while you count out thirty-seven cents. I'd like to mail you. Far, far away. You'd arrived damaged.

White Trash
GLORINE RITCHIE, APPALACHIA-BORN DIVORCÉE
AND ARSONIST'S WIFE

That cross tattoo on the wrist she got at fourteen didn't help her much. Her unfinished-looking fingertips rest on borrowed, cultured pearls, extracting purity, value, status, but only for a while, between inhales: her long, lit unfiltered cigarette is her best friend. It's patient, true-blue, sending its habitual ribbon of smoke snaking around the little defaced wrist. It's jewelry, too. Smoke goes with everything. Not like pearls, but like the song says, "Love the One You're With."

Designer and Manufacturer
IRIS BASCOMB AND DONNA TRUNT,
OWNER-OPERATORS OF WOMANART SILKSCREEN STUDIO

Yes, they're both women and they're holding hands. The one on top is long, unhappy, pampered, depressed. Years ago it was trained in ballet. Today it's creamed hysterically; weekly it's manicured, trimmed, shaped, professionally polished. Still, it lies around; there's nothing it wants to do.

The hand beneath is square, mechanically gifted, and rough. Abraded from dawn until dark with solvents, spirits, dryer, glaze, no fine qualities remain—just ink she can't wash out of the cuticles. *Cheese,* they say for the camera, their soft, curving semicircular smiles infatuated, cooperative.

Mud Slinger

FRANCINE MRZOZ, WELFARE LANDLORD

Rage bends the face of a Catholic farmer's widow into abstraction, a straight mouth, encroaching upward on shut eyes, blurred by action taken against an offense. Her palm rushes the lens, caked with mud that outlines its terrible, single line. The absence of complexity in the hand is worse than its absence in the face. Simplicity's one thing. This heart's criminal.

Romantic

VIOLA PLANJEK, LUNCHEONETTE OWNER

Slovenly, is your first thought. Excessive, your second. Her fingers are pudgy and bloated; her nails are savagely bitten. The flagrant, dark polish has been picked and chipped; all that remains is a few jagged flames. This hand, which has spent a lifetime rising trancelike to her mouth with things to drink or eat, including itself, is at rest now on a white palm with black edges. His upside-down nails are huge and strong, healthy and clean. They're younger than her. The trance ends here.

Resident Artist

ELEANOR HAFFEY, DAIRY FARMER'S WIFE
AND MOTHER OF EIGHT

She holds her own sketch askance, tipped away from view, rejecting it before it can reject her, the way she holds things in department stores—picking them up to see if she can afford them, knowing in advance the answer is no. The Saran Wrap she protected it with offers only glare. No art is visible, just large, coarse, beat-up knuckles. Joints unevenly swollen with arthritis from milking, a life of labor that began in willing innocence and never ended, the art equivalent of starvation.

Mom-and-Pop Insurance Agents

HELEN AND ROCKY SHURBERRY,
STATE FARM INSURANCE

Their hatred is choked and coughed in an endless, scratchy loop, horrible to listen to, but important, like a call-and-response work song recorded in the field at the dawn of recording. For forty-odd years, they shared one desk. Now they've retired to one cane. Their fingers tangle for supremacy in a naturally occurring pattern, like roots pushing their way around a rock. Sometimes he's on top, sometimes she. Where to go next: a single argument keeps them together.

Artificial Inseminator

DAVE L. GARSON, INC.

His face is as scary as a lit pumpkin as he points to the middle finger with its extra joint. It makes him the best in five counties. The animals don't know he's a nut; they let him do what he does. If it takes him longer than it should, they just flick a long tail his way and keep gumming hay. The extra joint is also good at working back doors. It's trickier. He has to catch them at the right time, say the right thing, exert a little pressure in the right place. Eventually, they'll moo.

Self-Made Woman

NORA JOHANSSEN, EXECUTIVE TELEVISION PRODUCER

It could be a mannequin's hand—it's that featureless, that broken, lying on the white sheet, but it's my sister in the ICU. The manicure survived the car accident without a scratch, though she's in a coma. In this hospital light, her palm looks lineless, her fingerprints erased. She left all her lines behind in my two hands when she left home. Now, we read her destiny in the lines of the monitor instead, a man-made deity we adore over and over for drawing the same green mountain.

Solicitor

JAMES BOSWELL, ATTORNEY AT LAW

It's tossed there in sleep, the left hand of a married man, splayed against his bare chest. It's more naked than he: the wedding ring is gone, revealing a pale band of untanned skin he can't remove. We feel the need to judge this hand. It's sensitive, artistic, reasonable, thorough—so thorough, the implicated photographer feels the need to snap this souvenir. We guess it's also punctual. The watch reads twenty to three.

Photographer

TAMARA JOHANSSEN, PHOTOGRAPHER

I raise my right hand in the mirror, exposing the whole truth, foretold by a palm reader long ago. "You lose people here," she said, noting the splintered Life line. Between the first two fingers, she showed me a comma, wide and deep. "These are ... men," she said, her tone making the plural matter.

At the edge of my hand, beneath the baby finger, she looks for markings. "There might be two children," she said. She didn't mention both would be lost, scraped free, sent back to God within sixty days. "You have a good head," she said, stroking the smile at the top of my palm. Then she tapped on the strange, crosshatched line beneath it, saying, "The heart needs work."

Sex, death, art—everything she warned me about lies in my palm as history. One event escaped her: the thin, healed slash along the wrist that carefully misses the big vein. It's there to testify. I am alive, it says, and all is somehow well.

Acknowledgments

For her vision, passion, and tenacity, I am indebted to my agent, Denise Shannon. For her insight, precision, and perfect pitch, I am indebted to my editor, Pat Strachan.

About the Author

Lucia Nevai's short fiction has been published in *The New Yorker,* *Zoetrope,* the *Iowa Review, New England Review,* and other period-icals. She is the author of two collections of stories, *Star Game,* which won the Iowa Short Fiction Award, and *Normal.* Born in Iowa, Nevai now lives in upstate New York.